When glass artist Marco Ravél is commissioned to create a piece for a rich recluse, he's thrilled for the opportunity to stretch his creative muscle. He doesn't expect to fall for the man hiring him. For Henrik Schweitzer, the relationship blossoming between himself and Marco shakes his world to its foundation. He wants to keep what the two of them have together, but after eight years of near-complete solitude he doesn't know if he has what it takes to change. Marco and Henrik both know they can have something special, if they can conquer the mountain of fears in their path.

MLR Press Authors

Featuring a roll call of some of the best writers of gay erotica and mysteries today!

Derek Adams	Z. Allora	Maura Anderson
Simone Anderson	Victor J. Banis	Laura Baumbach
Helen Beattie	Ally Blue	J.P. Bowie
Barry Brennessel	Nowell Briscoe	Jade Buchanan
James Buchanan	TA Chase	Charlie Cochrane
Karenna Colcroft	Michael G. Cornelius	Jamie Craig
Ethan Day	Diana DeRicci	Vivien Dean
Taylor V. Donovan	Theo Fenraven	S.J. Frost
Kimberly Gardner	Michael Gouda	Kaje Harper
Alex Ironrod	AC Katt	Thomas Kearnes
Sasha Keegan	Kiernan Kelly	K-lee Klein
Geoffrey Knight	Christopher Koehler	Matthew Lang
J.L. Langley	Vincent Lardo	Cameron Lawton
Anna Lee	Elizabeth Lister	Clare London
William Maltese	Z.A. Maxfield	Timothy McGivney
Tere Michaels	AKM Miles	Robert Moore
Reiko Morgan	Jet Mykles	William Neale
N.J. Nielsen	Cherie Noel	Gregory L. Norris
Willa Okati	Erica Pike	Neil S. Plakcy
Rick R. Reed	A.M. Riley	AJ Rose
Rob Rosen	George Seaton	Riley Shane
Jardonn Smith	DH Starr	Richard Stevenson
Liz Strange	Marshall Thornton	Lex Valentine
Haley Walsh	Mia Watts	Lynley Wayne
Missy Welsh	Ryal Woods	Stevie Woods
Lance Zarimba	Mark Zubro	

Check out titles, both available and forthcoming, at
www.mlrpress.com

The Mountain

Ally Blue

mlrpress
www.mlrpress.com

This book is a work of fiction. Names, characters, places, and incidents either are products of the author's imagination or are used fictitiously. Any resemblance to actual events or locales or persons, living or dead, is entirely coincidental.

Published by
MLR Press, LLC
3052 Gaines Waterport Rd.
Albion, NY 14411

Visit ManLoveRomance Press, LLC on the Internet:
www.mlrpress.com

Cover Art by Winterheart Designs
Editing by Kris Jacen

Print ISBN#978-1-60820-765-7
Ebook ISBN# 978-1-60820-764-0
Issued 2012

To Mama Kris, this plot bunny's baby daddy. Trust me, it makes sense. She planted the seed.

Chapter One

As soon as the blonde with the big tits and the too-short-for-the-weather skirt walked into his shop, Marco Ravél knew he was in trouble.

Not on his own account. Tits had never done it for him. Washboard abs, a rock-hard ass and a hint of five o'clock shadow were more his speed.

No, the trouble would come from Marco's shop assistant, Darryl. The kid had way more self-confidence than sense and Marco figured he could safely bet every dollar in the register that Darryl would be trying to tap that the minute he spotted it.

Because Furnace Glassworks had only been open for six months and couldn't afford to lose customers to Darryl's overactive sex drive, Marco brushed at his shirt in case of stray lunch crumbs and hurried toward the woman while Darryl was busy ringing up the old lady buying Christmas ornaments. As he rounded the big table in the middle of the shop where he'd displayed his glass sculptures, the woman lifted her phone and snapped a photo of the vase she'd been studying.

Marco frowned as the woman tapped at her phone, then started talking to someone through her headset. What the hell? Yeah, the vase kicked ass—tall, lush and curvy as the woman herself, formed from a gorgeous, smoky gray glass streaked with threads of vivid blue. One of his best, if he said so himself. But a picture? Uh-uh. Buy it or live without, that was Marco's motto.

He couldn't *say* that, though, much as he might want to. Just because someone didn't buy this time didn't mean they wouldn't next time.

Deep breath, hot head. Be cool.

Nodding to himself, he forced his face into its most pleasant smile and strolled up to the lady with the body, the expensive outfit and the camera phone. "Good afternoon, ma'am. Anything

I can help you with?"

She looked up at him—not far up; her heels put her within a couple of inches of his six foot two—and flashed a dazzling smile. "Yes, in fact you can. I think I'd like to buy this vase." She glanced down at her phone. "Right? What do you think?"

Her headset kept Marco from hearing whatever the person on the other end of the line said, but her smile came back a couple of seconds later and the big blue eyes raised to meet his again.

Damn, she was good. If he'd swung that way he'd have drooled.

He gave her his best cool eyebrow arch. "Did you decide?"

"Yes. I'll definitely take it." Murmuring something Marco didn't quite catch—presumably to the mystery person on the other end of her headset—she stuck her phone into a holder on the waistband of her skirt. "Could you wrap it for me, please?"

"Sure." Very carefully, he lifted the vase and carried it to the checkout counter. Hot Blonde followed him, her heels practically noiseless on the short carpet he'd installed because the thought of a wood floor under all that glass gave him the screaming heebie-jeebies. "What sort of occasion is it? We have pretty much any kind of paper you might want. You can get a card next door at Dottie's."

She laughed. Of course her laugh had to fit the rest of her—so pretty it was kind of ridiculous. "No, I didn't mean like that. It's not for any occasion." Setting a red leather purse on the counter, she unzipped it and pulled out a matching wallet. "It's just that I still have a lot to do this afternoon, then I have about an hour's drive to get home. I'd like the vase wrapped to make sure it doesn't break, that's all." She handed him a credit card. "It's a beautiful piece."

"Thank you." He took the card, then hesitated. "Don't you want to know how much it is?"

"Not really. I want it no matter what it costs." She smiled, looking amused. "Thanks for checking, though."

Yeah, me and my big mouth. He swiped the card. It cleared, of course. People who didn't care about price never had their plastic denied. It was a law of the jungle or something.

He handed the card back, along with the slip for her to sign. She took the piece of paper and scribbled her name on the line. "So. Do you make all these pieces yourself, Mr. Ravél?"

Startled, he blinked at her. "How do you know my name?"

"It's on your business card." She nodded at the stack of them sitting in front of the register.

"Oh. Yeah." He took the signed credit card slip she handed him. "How'd you know I'm Marco Ravél, though?"

Her perfectly shaped brows rose. "I'm a businesswoman. I know an owner when I see one."

Marco laughed. "Okay, I'll buy that. So, yeah, I make all the things in the shop."

"Hm."

Whether that was a good *hm* or a bad one, Marco had no clue, so he kept quiet. Fetching a box and a pile of tissue paper from the shelf behind the checkout counter, he got busy wrapping the vase Augustina Pryce—according to her Visa—had just bought. He couldn't help noticing she picked up one of his business cards and put it in her purse.

Once the vase was safely packed in a box with tissue paper and newspapers for extra padding, Marco put it in a sturdy bag and handed it across the counter to her. "There you go, Ms. Pryce. Enjoy your vase, and thank you for shopping at Furnace Glassworks. I hope we'll see you here again."

"Oh, you might." She studied him with an uncomfortably keen interest. "Do you ever work on commission?"

"Sometimes." He smiled, trying to play it cool and not look as curious as he felt. "Do you have a piece you need done?"

"Not at the moment. But I might, in the future." There went the toothpaste-commercial smile again. "Thank you, Mr. Ravél. Maybe I'll see you again soon."

"Come by any time."

After she'd left the shop, Marco planted his palms on the counter and let his smile relax into the *what just fucking happened* expression fighting to get out. For once, he was glad of the unseasonably chilly weather keeping the tourists off the sidewalks and thus out of the shop. He needed a minute alone to think. His little store had done all right so far. A large percentage of Gatlinburg's hundreds of thousands of tourists were looking to buy unique, locally made artwork as gifts or mementos of their stay. His glass art fit the bill, and he'd done a respectable business since he'd opened in November, just in time for the holiday travel boom. Still, making a living this way was harder than it sounded. A good commission could net him a whole lot more profit, a whole lot faster.

An elbow in his ribs brought him out of his thoughts. He straightened up and faced Darryl. "I don't have her number, so don't ask."

Darryl grinned, not a bit fazed. "It's cool. You can introduce me when she comes back." He clapped Marco on the shoulder with one big, solid hand, and sauntered toward the door to greet the trio of well-heeled older women who'd just entered.

Marco shook his head, smiling in spite of himself. If Augustina Pryce *did* come back, he'd damn well introduce her to Darryl. He needed a woman ten times smarter than him to take him down a few notches.

While his assistant charmed the customers, Marco went back to his workshop to find something to replace the vase on the sales floor. Maybe he'd end up with a commission and maybe he wouldn't. In the meantime, he had a business to run.

§ § §

To Henrik Schweitzer, nothing topped the beauty of a Tennessee mountain sunrise, especially when viewed from the hot tub in the courtyard he'd come to think of as his, since it was outside his suite.

He smiled as the morning's first light spilled over the peaks and valleys falling from the old family estate to the town of Gatlinburg still sleeping far below. The winter had been harsh, with more snow than Henrik could remember since his parents had sent him to live here with his grandparents, when he was a child. The spring leaves coated the folds of the land in a bright green mist, and more birds sang in the branches every morning. It lifted his spirits, in spite of the temperatures still hovering in the mid-thirties each day when he came outside for his pre-dawn hot tub soak.

He loved spring. Loved the new foliage, the flowers, the buzz of bees everywhere. Most of all, he loved being able to get outside into the forest. To wander the woods around the estate. Explore the land he'd known and loved forever. Once he'd gotten lost and slept in a cave, and he hadn't even been frightened.

Unlike the one time he'd let Gus talk him into going into town with her.

The mere memory made him queasy. She'd been so angry with him. He'd been angry with himself. More so because he knew it would be the same if he could do it over. He'd panic, run away and curl up in a corner of the men's room shaking and crying just like before, because he couldn't control it.

Neither of them had understood his disease then. They both did now. Which was why Gus still lived here with him.

Henrik waited until the sun's disc cleared the treetops, then he rose from the hot tub, took his towel from the chair and headed inside while drying himself. Gus had probably gotten in late—she usually did when she went into town—but she would've left Henrik's new vase in his sitting room for him. He was anxious to see it in person, as it were.

Sure enough, when he went from his bedroom to his sitting room he instantly spotted the vase on his coffee table. It was even more stunning in real life, its curves almost feminine in their heartbreaking beauty. The streaks of brilliant blue in the gray glass accented the shape of the vase, giving it a sense of motion in a way Henrik couldn't quite define.

He loved it. *Loved* it. Maybe more than any other piece in his extensive art collection.

Throwing the wet towel on the floor, he strode naked toward the sitting room door. He didn't hold out much hope for Gus being up yet, but you never knew. If by some miracle she'd woken early today, he had an immediate need to find out more about the artist who'd created his vase, and whether he might be able to commission a piece from said artist. If Gus was still asleep—most likely the case—he'd make coffee. Maybe make the hazelnut cinnamon rolls he'd looked up the recipe for online last night in a fit of culinary creativity.

If that didn't get Gus out of bed, nothing would.

§ § §

Apparently, nothing would coax Gus out of bed this morning. Henrik finally gave up by the time the cinnamon rolls came out of the oven. He poured a second cup of coffee, put a hot cinnamon roll on a plate and sat at the breakfast bar to eat. Granola or yogurt would've been healthier, but his sweet tooth wouldn't take no for an answer this morning. Besides, he'd work it off later. The day promised to be perfect for a trail run.

He'd just popped the last bite into his mouth when he heard the telltale faint squeak of the second to the last step on the back stairs, which led from the second floor to the big breakfast room behind him. "Cinnamon rolls're in the oven," he called without turning around as soon as he heard the shuffle of bare feet on the wood floor. "I'll be merciful and wait until you have coffee before I ask you about the glass artist."

"Well, I don't know what the deal is with the glass artist, and I don't drink coffee, but I love cinnamon rolls."

Henrik's pulse rose and his back tensed at the sound of the unexpected, unfamiliar male voice. Not that it was completely unheard of, but Gus hadn't brought home a man in *months*. Henrik had gotten used to being able to wander into the kitchen naked in the morning without the risk of running into some guy he didn't know.

Sighing, Henrik swiveled to face whoever his cousin had chosen to spend the night with. He was surprisingly scruffy—not Gus's usual type at all—but the glint in his eyes and the mischievous tilt of his smile said he was adventurous in bed. That was *definitely* Gus's type.

Henrik forced a smile. "Help yourself. There's plenty."

"Cool. Thanks, man." Tall, Scruffy and Adventurous shuffled to the oven, opened it, took out a cinnamon roll and took a healthy bite. He leaned against the counter in his clingy purple boxer-briefs and watched Henrik with interest while he chewed. He swallowed and wiped his mouth. "So. Who're you?" He leaned sideways. "And why're you naked?"

"That's my cousin Henrik. He's always naked because he's weird." Gus walked into the kitchen wearing her favorite oversized Bugs Bunny T-shirt, her hair caught up in a tangled ponytail. Yawning, she went to the man in the purple underwear and kissed the corner of his admittedly-kissable mouth. "Rikky, this is Lance." She pointed at him before he could say, *I know.* "Not a word."

He widened his eyes. She rolled hers and went for the coffee pot.

Lance glanced from Gus to Henrik and back with a frown, but didn't ask. Smart guy. No man ever wanted to hear that he was at least the seventh Lance to christen his one-night-stand's expensive sheets. Henrik had no clue why Gus only brought home Lances and took the other men to hotels, but he hardly had room to talk about anyone else's quirks when he hadn't left his property in almost eight years and rarely wore clothes anymore except when hiking or running through the woods.

Since Lance showed no signs of being scared off by Henrik's presence, he decided to make an effort at conversation in spite of the beginnings of anxiety making him fidget. He clutched his coffee mug tighter. "So, Lance. How did you and Gus meet?"

Gus scowled. Lance's eyebrows shot up. "Gus?"

"It's short for Augustina. Rikky's the only one who calls me that." Gus shot him a fond smile—rare for her this early in the morning—grabbed a cinnamon roll from the oven and leaned against the counter. "Private party. You know the Tomlinsons, right?"

Henrik nodded. Not that he'd ever met them in person, unless you counted the times they'd come to visit his parents when he was very small, but he knew *of* them. "Tara and Toni having another 'business meeting'?"

Gus laughed. The twin girls had pretty much taken over the family's chain of successful wine shops, using it as an excuse for the constant parties they dubbed *business meetings,* so they could write them off on their taxes. "Yep. They were trying out some products from a couple of new wineries they were thinking of carrying." She took a bite of her cinnamon roll. "Mmm. Hazelnut. Good."

"Thanks." Henrik sipped his coffee. "Nobody else calls me Rikky, by the way. Just as a reminder. So, we're even."

Gus peered at him with the full force of the frightening intelligence Henrik didn't think any of the men she bedded ever recognized. He smiled to show her that yes, he knew quite well no one but her ever called him anything because no one else ever saw him or talked to him. No one but their dwindling, scattered family even knew he existed.

Which was no one's fault but his own, of course. He accepted that. He'd made his peace with it. Gus still held out hope for him, though. She hated his loneliness and hated even more that she couldn't fix it. He suspected that was why she was so willing to help him indulge his art habit.

The tightness eased from Gus's expression and she smiled, blue eyes warm. "Yeah, I guess we're even." She took a long swallow of coffee and turned toward Lance. "Sorry if this seems abrupt, Lance, but Rikky and I have a lot of business we need to take care of today, so I'm going to need you to clear out after breakfast."

He grinned. "Hot, tiger in the sack, *and* no strings after. I like it." He popped the last bite of cinnamon roll into his mouth, chewed and swallowed. "Last night was awesome. Call me if you want to do it again sometime. You've got my number."

"Sure thing. I had a great time too." She pushed away from the counter and went into Lance's arms for a long, deep kiss. "We have water bottles in the fridge if you want one."

"Cool, thanks." Lance patted her on the ass, drew away and went to the refrigerator to get a bottle of Henrik's vitamin water. "See you, Gus." He saluted Henrik with the bottle. "Nice to meet you, Rikky."

"You too, Lance." Henrik waved at Lance as he headed up the stairs to get dressed. "Nice guy."

"He's not a jerk, he has a great dick and he knows what to do with a pussy. I have no complaints." She gulped from her coffee mug, then went to the pot for more. "Not clingy either. This is a very good thing in my book."

Henrik shook his head. "Are you sure you're not a gay man trapped in a woman's body?"

She shot him the look she'd perfected ages ago to make people feel one inch tall and stupid. Lucky for him, Henrik had been best friends with her all his life, and was immune. He grinned, and she laughed. "You're such an ass."

"Yet you love me anyway." He drained his mug, held it out toward Gus and wiggled it. "As long as you have the pot, please?"

She crossed to where he sat and filled his mug. "So, what'd you think of the vase?" Setting the coffee pot on the counter, she leaned on her elbows and watched his face.

"It's incredible. Even better than the picture." He put his free hand over hers and squeezed. "Thanks, Gus."

"My pleasure, as always. Art shopping is fun." She smiled, showing the faint dimple in her left cheek. "The glass artist was very hot, by the way."

"Oh yeah?" Henrik picked up the cinnamon crumbs from his plate and sucked them off his finger. "What'd he look like? Or was it a she?"

"A he, dummy. Why else would I even mention it? His name is Marco Ravél. He is tall, dark, and handsome. Italian, maybe? Hang on." Leaving her mug on the counter, she ran down the hallway to the front of the house and returned a moment later with her purse. She fished out her iPhone, turned it on and started thumbing through her photos. When she found the one she wanted, she held it out to him. "Here. See for yourself."

Henrik took the phone with a laugh. "I can't believe he let you take a picture of him."

"He didn't know."

"Yeah, that sounds more like you."

Henrik looked at the photo, and whistled. The picture only showed the man from the chest up and was slightly blurry, probably on account of it being taken in secret, but it was clear enough for Henrik to make out the large, dark eyes, the wide, sensual mouth, and the slightly crooked nose that looked like it had been broken at some point. Close-cropped dark hair showed every muscle and tendon in what looked like a strong neck. Henrik thought he caught the glint of piercings in the man's nose, eyebrow and ears.

Henrik licked his lips. Pierced and artsy wasn't his usual type—not that he had a type, really, other than in online porn—but he couldn't deny his urge to tear the shirt off Marco Ravél's wide shoulders and see if the rest of his body looked as tough, wiry and dangerously sexy as his face and neck.

The idea of asking Gus to use her considerable feminine wiles on the man to get *those* sorts of pictures popped into Henrik's head and got firmly trounced by the sensible parts of him before his long-caged libido could take control of his tongue, and make it ask.

Unfortunately, Gus knew him every bit as well as he knew her. She snickered as soon as he handed her phone back to her. "Sorry, that's all I'm ever going to get as far as pictures. He plays for your team."

And damned if the man didn't just become ten times as intriguing. Not to mention a thousand times as terrifying. Henrik cupped his mug in both hands. "How do you know that?"

She gave him an *I can't believe I have to explain this to you* look. "Rik. Honey. He didn't look at me like a *woman*, he looked at me like a piece of artwork. He knew I was beautiful, but he wasn't feeling it like a man." Laying her phone on the counter, she picked up her coffee and sipped. "Trust me, when you've seen that *I want to fuck you* look enough times, you know when the look you're getting from a man isn't that one."

Henrik laughed. "I'll take your word for it."

She pinned him with a skull-drilling stare. "You are a stunningly good-looking man, Rikky. You could have any man you wanted, if you just—"

"You've said." He hunched forward, letting his hair fall over his eyes to hide from her gaze. Not for the first time, he wished he had Gus's thick honey-blonde curls instead of the near-white, stick-straight strands too thin and fine to provide a true shield from his cousin's laser death stare. "I've tried, okay? The last time I left the estate was a disaster. I don't even want to anymore. I'm fine here by myself." He peered through the veil of his overly long bangs at Gus's frown. "I have you."

"Always. You know that. I love living here." She leaned forward to rest her head against his. "It's not enough, though, honey. You have to know that. One day, it's not going to be enough for you."

He didn't say anything, because she was right and he knew it. He wanted love. Companionship. A man to share his life. He wanted a *life*, a normal life. God, he wanted it, but he knew he'd never have that unless he could overcome his crippling fear of the world Outside. And he had no idea how to do that. The psychiatrists he'd seen years ago hadn't helped. Trial by fire hadn't helped. Nothing had helped. So here he was, twenty-seven years old, rich as sin, and resigned to a life alone.

He stroked her hair. "I don't know why you stay with me, Gus. But I'm glad you do. I love you."

"That's why I stay with you, stupid. Because I love you too. More than anything in the world." She planted a kiss on his forehead, then straightened up, her eyes suspiciously shiny. "Hey, I asked Mister Sexy Glass Artist if he does commissions, and he said he does. So if you want more of his work, just let me know. I'll go back and hire him."

A commission. His own personalized artwork by the gorgeous, *gay* glass artist an hour or so away down the mountain in Gatlinburg. The thought was enough to heat Henrik's cheeks and kick his pulse into high gear, though he couldn't have said why, exactly.

Gus grinned, and Henrik cursed his ultra-pale German skin for about the hundred millionth time. God, he'd give anything to control his tendency to blush, even if no one but Gus ever saw it.

Gathering his dignity around him as best he could, he sat up straight and shook his hair out of his eyes. "You know, I think that's a great idea. I've been meaning to replace the chandelier in the formal dining room for ages. I think a glass art piece would be perfect in there."

"It absolutely would. I'll head back into town tomorrow and work out a deal with him." Smiling ear to ear, Gus took her coffee and went to fetch the rest of her cinnamon roll from where she'd left it beside the coffee pot. "All right, I'm going to shower and dress. I have a video conference with the VPs in a couple of hours. And don't forget, *you* need to call Carl this afternoon at two-thirty. Just to touch base, that's all." She patted his shoulder on her way to the stairs. "Don't worry, I have everything under control. Carl's insecure, you know that. Let him know he has your ear and he'll be fine."

Henrik wrinkled his nose. He hated video conferences with the president of his parents' company, but as the nominal owner he had a duty to stay in touch. "Yeah, I know. Thanks."

"Don't forget to put on a suit."

For a second, Henrik considered showing up to video conference in his birthday suit. Poor Carl would probably have a stroke.

Gus turned at the bottom of the steps and glared at Henrik as if she knew what he was thinking. He gave her his sweetest smile. "My dark gray Armani, with the pale gray shirt and the lavender tie. What do you think?"

"Professional, but friendly. It'll put Carl at ease. Approved." She arched an eyebrow at him before hurrying up the steps toward her suite of rooms on the second floor.

Chuckling to himself, Henrik rose from the barstool and went to empty the coffee pot into his mug. He had a whole day ahead of him. Maybe he could have another soak in his hot tub while he planned his commission for Sexy Glass Artist.

If he spent a little time thinking about the artist himself, Henrik didn't think anyone would blame him.

Chapter Two

Marco had barely gotten his newest creation—a slim, graceful pitcher with a bare hint of pale green shading the clear glass—into the annealing oven when Darryl burst through the workshop door. "Phone, Marco."

"Okay, hang on." Marco pulled off his insulated gloves and crossed to where his assistant stood holding the smart phone Marco had bought when he opened his store. "Business or personal?"

"It's that hot girl that was in here the other day, and she wants to talk to *you*." Darryl grinned, making him look like the college boy he still was at heart. "I'd say that makes it business."

"Hilarious. Don't ditch the day job."

Darryl *pfft*ed. Shaking his head, Marco took the phone. "This is Marco."

"Hello, Marco. This is Augustina Pryce. I bought the blue and gray vase on Wednesday, do you remember?"

"I sure do." Marco grabbed a towel from the rack beside the door and mopped sweat from his head. "How are you?"

"I'm doing very well, thank you. And you?"

"Doing great, thanks." *Out*, Marco mouthed at Darryl, hitching a thumb toward the shop. Darryl scowled but left, thank God. Marco didn't want to lose any business because Darryl was more interested in listening in on phone conversations than selling glass art. "So, what can I help you with today, Ms. Pryce?"

"Augustina, please." She cleared her throat. It made her sound nervous, something Marco wouldn't have expected from her. He waited, curious. "Actually, I wonder if you might have time to meet me for lunch. I have something I'd like to discuss with you."

Lunch?

He glanced at the clock before he even thought about it, as if the time was actually a factor here. Although eleven o'clock was a great time to get lunch in this town. Early enough to beat the crowds.

He gave himself a mental shake. Augustina Pryce was clearly an intelligent woman, and an observant one. No way would she have mistaken him for straight. "Lunch sounds great. Did you have someplace in mind?"

"How about Smoky's, on the Parkway? It's one of my favorite places in town."

Marco grinned at the phone. He'd been afraid she'd pick some fancy-ass place with square plates, appetizer-size portions of shit he'd never heard of, and enormous prices. Smoky's Sports Pub & Grub wasn't what he'd expected a rich woman to pick, but hell, he'd take it. Their wings kicked ass.

"It's one of my favorite places too, as a matter of fact." He trailed his fingers through the sweat running down his bare chest. "I've been working in the hot shop, so I'll need to shower and change, but I can meet you there in, say, half an hour? Does that work for you?"

"That'll be perfect. I'll see you then, Marco."

"Looking forward to it."

The connection broke. Marco stuck the phone in his back pocket and stared at the big metal tool chest against the wall. She hadn't said so, but he had a feeling he was about to get a commission. Hopefully a lucrative one. It'd been a while since he'd created a piece on commission. He'd missed the unique challenge of it.

Grinning, he went to tell Darryl he was in charge of the shop for the next two or three hours.

§ § §

Fifteen minutes later, Marco locked his apartment above the shop, hurried down the back stairs and set off to walk the half mile to Smoky's. He glanced up at the overcast sky. The forecast only called for a slight chance of rain, and the clouds didn't look particularly threatening, but still. The last thing he wanted was to show up at what might be an important business meeting looking like a drowned rat.

Too bad he'd never gotten around to replacing his broken umbrella. He'd never cared that much about getting wet before.

A sunbeam broke through the solid gray overhead to light the leather goods store across the street in gold for a few seconds. Taking it as a sign, Marco stuck his hands in his jacket pockets and picked up his pace.

As he expected, he made it to Smoky's without getting rained on. Augustina was already there, sitting at a table at the back of the room and studying a menu. She wore black slacks this time, with a snug pale blue sweater that showed her cleavage. She looked up and smiled as he approached. "Hi, Marco. I'm so glad you could meet with me today. Please, sit down."

"Thanks. It's great to see you." Marco parked himself in the chair across from her, opened his menu and pretended deep interest in its contents. "I'm in the mood for some wings today. What about it? Want to split an order? The one pound makes a perfect appetizer for two."

"That sounds wonderful. I like them hot, if that's all right with you."

"Hell, yeah. Follow that up with the blackened trout and a bottle of chardonnay?" Marco shut his eyes and kissed his fingertips. "Heaven."

When he opened his eyes, Augustina was grinning at him. "You struck me as more of a beer type."

"Yeah, well. You struck me as more of a square-plate type. I guess we surprised each other."

She laughed. "I guess we did, at that." She rested her elbows on the table. "I have to suffer through plenty of 'square plate' restaurants in the name of my family's business. Those places get really old after a while. I'd much rather relax and enjoy myself, even when I'm talking business."

The moment of truth. Marco smiled at her, doing his best not to look too eager. "Like now?"

"Right you are." Augustina beckoned one of the waiters over. "Hi. Danny, right?"

"Yeah." The boy gave her a love-struck smile. "Are you ready to order?"

"We are, yes." She pointed at the menu. "We're going to have a one pound order of hot wings to start, and a bottle of chardonnay. And I'm going to have the mango salmon platter."

"Mango salmon. Okay." Danny finished jotting down Augustina's order, then turned wide brown eyes to Marco. "And for you, sir?"

Sir. Damn, that was equal parts cute and hot. Good thing the kid looked legal or Marco might've felt bad for the impure thoughts he was having right now.

He favored the boy with a bright smile which probably sailed right over his head, since he kept cutting sidelong glances at Augustina's boobs. "I'll have the mountain trout. Blackened."

Danny scribbled on his order pad, the tip of his tongue sticking out at the corner of his mouth. Marco looked at the table instead.

After Danny gathered the menus and left, Marco lifted his gaze to find Augustina grinning at him. *Busted.* He raised his eyebrows. "What?"

"Nothing." She put on a more serious expression, though the amused glint in her eyes told Marco she'd indeed caught him looking. Not that it mattered, really. "I know your time is valuable, Marco, so I'll get to the point. The vase I bought the other day was for my cousin, Henrik. He collects all sorts of art. He loved your vase so much that he asked me to commission you to create a glasswork chandelier for our formal dining room."

A commission. From a rich person.

Marco managed not to jump up and run around the place whooping like a football fan whose team had just won the Super

Bowl, but it was a near thing, even though he'd been expecting it. He clasped his hands on the table and nodded thoughtfully. "I'd be very interested in that, yes. I'd need to see the space, of course."

She gave him a look that said she saw right through his false calm, but she kept that to herself. "Of course. I have some photos with me on my phone, so you can get a sense of it right away. We can make an appointment for you to come by the estate and see it in person whenever you have time. I have engagements of my own, of course, but my schedule is flexible for the most part. I'll do everything I can to work around yours."

"I appreciate that. Thank you."

A woman approached with a bottle of chardonnay in one hand and two wineglasses in the other. She set them all on the table with a smile. "Hi, folks. I'm Sharon, I'll be serving your wine today."

"Wonderful. Thank you, Sharon." Augustina blinked up at the other woman. "Danny isn't old enough, huh?"

Sharon let out a raspy laugh. "Still a good nine months short of twenty-one." She pulled a corkscrew out of her apron pocket and twisted it into the wine cork with a practiced hand. "He's a good kid, though. Smart as a whip." Tugging the cork free of the bottle, she poured each glass half full, set the bottle down and recorked it. "All right, folks. Anything I can get you?"

Marco glanced at Augustina, who shook her head. He smiled at Sharon. "We're fine, thanks."

"Okay. Give me or Danny a yell if you need anything."

She bustled off to check on another table. Marco picked up his wine glass and took a sip. "Mm. Good."

"Yes. I like their featured brand." Augustina sipped from her wine as well.

They sat in silence for a moment. Marco eyed Augustina's phone, lying innocently on the table. He wanted to see, she'd offered to show him, so…

He nodded toward the phone. "Would you mind if I went ahead and looked at the photos of your dining room now?"

"Not at all. I'll bring them up." She picked up her phone, fiddled with it for a second, and handed it across the table to him. "Here… I'm not sure how many photos there are of the dining room, but they're all together. You'll know when you come to the end of them."

Marco took the phone. He whistled when he saw the first picture. "Wow. Very nice."

"Thank you." She smiled. "My grandparents built the house when they got married. Henrik and I grew up there."

Marco got the feeling there was a truly fascinating story behind that one sentence, but since she didn't offer to elaborate he didn't ask. He turned his attention back to the pictures instead, studying each one closely as he scrolled through them.

Augustina had done a thorough job of documenting the space. And what a space it was. It was large but not *too* large, with dark hardwood floors. A long wooden table, simple but obviously old and expensive, ran down the middle of the room, a bouquet of calla lilies in a clear crystal vase acting as a centerpiece. Eight equally simple matching chairs surrounded it. Natural light poured in through three tall arched windows in one of the short walls. A matching arched doorway in the opposite wall opened into what looked like a butler's pantry. Beadboard walls painted a soft taupe climbed at least nine feet to a graceful ivory crown molding and matching ivory ceiling. Sheer ivory curtains hung open over the windows, flowing from wrought iron rods that looked custom-made. The sideboard along one of the long walls matched the table. Several pieces of silver sat on top.

Marco saw instantly why they'd decided to replace the existing light fixture. The standard candelabra chandelier wasn't completely out of place in the traditional room, but it did nothing to accent the serene beauty of the space either.

His mind already running through ideas for the new light fixture, Marco flipped to the next photo. And stopped, staring.

This wasn't the dining room. It must've been the same house, though. Marco spotted the same hardwood floors, beadboard walls and arched windows in the background. But the foreground was the part that stole his voice and paralyzed him with his mouth hanging open like an idiot. Marco didn't generally go for blonds, but damn, he'd make an exception for the man in the photo—ice-blue eyes, cut-glass jaw, lips specially created for sucking cock. And the *body,* God. The man was Marco's walking wet dream, from the beautifully formed shoulders down the hard bare chest to the perfectly cut V leading into the tiny, low-hanging shorts. The man had one hand held out, smiling, as if trying to tell the girl with the camera not to take his picture. He looked a lot like Augustina, but he gave off an indefinable air of vulnerability that his cousin most certainly didn't.

Marco licked his lips, because he couldn't help it. Hopefully Augustina would forgive him. "This must be Henrik."

She didn't even reach for the phone to look, which made Marco even more curious about her and Henrik than he already was. "That's him, yes." She lifted her wine glass and took a sip, watching him over the rim. "That's the end of the dining room pics, then."

"Yeah." Marco thought about paging through another picture or three in hopes of seeing more of Henrik, but figured he'd never get away with it. He handed Augustina her phone. "The shop's usually slow on Sunday mornings. Would that be a good time for me to come by and check out the dining room?"

"That would be fine. I'll email you directions."

Danny arrived with their order of wings at that moment. The conversation turned to small talk as they tackled the food. Through the whole thing, though, Marco couldn't get the image of his companion's hot cousin out of his head.

Thinking of the suspiciously triumphant smile on Augustina's face, Marco couldn't help thinking she'd planned it that way.

He drained his wineglass and poured himself a refill. Sunday ought to be fun.

§ § §

Henrik planned on a weight room workout Sunday morning. He'd spent part of Saturday doing laundry and housework—he and Gus didn't employ a household staff—and the rest lazing around in his courtyard, reading, so he felt a particular need for exercise today. But by nine a.m. the temperatures had climbed into the low sixties and the clouds had parted to let the sun shine on the leaves and budding flowers.

He couldn't make himself stay indoors on such a morning. Leaving a note for Gus on the kitchen table, he pulled on shorts, a tank top and his favorite running shoes and headed outside.

He took the trail that circled his grandparents' property in a huge loop. Expansive vistas opened on first one side of the trail, then the other, offering alternating views of the house and gardens and the Smoky Mountain wilderness. The back section of the loop offered a gorgeous view of Gatlinburg in its valley below.

Henrik returned from his run feeling relaxed, refreshed and centered in body and mind, just as he always did. Tossing his sweat-soaked shirt into the mudroom hamper on the way in, he grabbed a towel from the shelf. He kicked his shoes into the corner, peeled off his socks and shorts—which also went into the hamper—and wandered toward the kitchen, drying himself as he went.

Going to the refrigerator, he opened it, took out an orange-flavored vitamin water, twisted off the cap and gulped a third of it in one breath. He set down the bottle with a deep sigh and wiped his mouth. Nothing tasted as good as cold water after an hour-plus run.

Looking around, he noticed coffee had been made, half the carafe already gone. So Gus was up and around, someplace. Slinging his towel over his shoulder, Henrik crossed the kitchen to pour himself a cup of coffee. He didn't think he could drink it straight from the pot right now, but he'd learned long ago that if he left it in the freezer for the few minutes it took him to shower, he could pour it over ice, mix with some cold milk and have himself a perfect iced coffee.

He was filling a plastic to-go mug with coffee when he heard his cousin's laughter from the direction of the dining room, followed by her voice saying something Henrik couldn't make out. Frowning, he set the mug down and padded over to the door to see what was up. They hosted very few functions here these days—none of which Henrik attended, for obvious reasons—and they certainly didn't have a party planned this morning. So what the heck was Gus doing talking to herself in there?

He froze when he heard a man's voice. *Crap. She did it again.*

The voices were coming closer. Through the butler's pantry, toward the kitchen.

Irritated, Henrik leaned against the counter and crossed his arms over his chest. He left the towel hanging over his shoulder instead of wrapping it around his hips. If Gus was going to keep on bringing home her one-night-Lances, they could just damn well get used to a naked Henrik in the kitchen. This was *his* house too.

Gus walked into the kitchen, talking over her shoulder to the man following her. She stopped when she saw Henrik. "Oh. Hi, Rikky."

He had a smooth, snarky greeting all set to go. But it got stuck somewhere between his brain and his mouth, because the man who trailed behind Gus wasn't a Lance. He wasn't just some guy who Henrik could shock with his nudity and never lay eyes on again.

It was Marco Ravél. The glass artist.

Crap.

Chapter Three

Someone was speaking to him.

Gus.

Gus was talking, but her words slid straight through Henrik's mind without imprinting, because the artist was staring at him with dark eyes full of something that made him feel pinned to the wall, his pulse rushing in his ears.

That penetrating gaze slid down, the tip of the man's tongue came out to wet his lips, and rising panic kicked Henrik into action. He whipped his towel off his shoulder and held it in front of his crotch with both hands. "Um. Okay. I, I'm—"

"Rikky. Hey. It's all right." Gus came forward, touched his shoulder and gave him a worried look. "I could've sworn I told you Marco was coming over this morning, but I guess I forgot. I'm sorry."

Marco rubbed a hand on the back of his neck and glanced around the room, obviously uncomfortable and doing his best to look anywhere but at Henrik. "I'm sorry too, man. I never would've come in here if I'd've known you were…" He waved a hand toward Henrik. "Well. You know."

"Yeah." Henrik laughed. It didn't sound too hysterical, which he thought was pretty great, considering the rapid gallop of his heart at this point and how hard his knees shook. "I, uh, I'm s-sorry we had to meet like this, Marco, but it *is* nice to meet you, regardless." He glanced at his towel with a faint smile. "You'll excuse me if I don't shake hands."

Marco's mouth curved into a wicked grin that did all sorts of interesting things to Henrik's insides. "Naw, that's fine. Maybe next time." The deep brown eyes stared into Henrik's once more, making his cheeks heat. "I'm very happy to meet you too, Henrik. No matter how it happened."

Henrik swallowed. He'd never before been in the physical

presence of a man to whom he was attracted. The reality of it—the movement of Marco's body, the way his mouth shaped words, even the obvious strength of his hands and his deep, rumbling voice—made Henrik feel hot inside. Made his balls tingle and begin to tighten. His cock started to rise under the towel. God, if he didn't get out of here fast he was going to embarrass himself in more ways than simple nudity in front of someone he'd probably have to interact with more than once.

He backed away, his gaze fixed on Marco Ravél. "I need to go. I n-need to shower and dress. Thanks. For doing my dining room." Unable to bear it any longer, he turned and fled.

His last glimpse of the artist's startled but pleased expression went with him, as did the guilty but undeniably satisfied look on Gus's face.

So Gus had planned this little encounter. Maybe not the naked part—he didn't think she'd do that to him deliberately—but definitely the meeting part. She knew Henrik would make himself scarce if he'd known they had company coming.

Back in the privacy of his suite, Henrik gave up on trying to hide the lust burning in his gut. He opened the bottom drawer of his bedside table, took out the slim, vibrating butt plug he'd bought online and the bottle of self-warming lube, then spread the towel on the bed and lay down.

When he came with the plug in his ass and his slick hand wrapped around his erection, it was to the imagined feel of the artist's hands on his body, the artist's mouth on his, the artist's cock moving deep inside him.

He stared at the ceiling, spent, sticky, and terrified for no reason he could pinpoint. Tears welled up, blurring his vision.

He let them come. There was no one to see.

§ § §

The first thing Marco thought when he saw Gus's cousin standing there in the kitchen, naked as the day he was born, was that the picture didn't do him justice. Not by a long shot. It didn't capture the sculpted perfection of his tapered waist, slim hips and lean, hard-muscled thighs, or the way his damp hair brushed the curve of his shoulders and clung to his neck. Most of all, the picture didn't come close to catching the glow of his bare skin in the morning sunlight, or the complete lack of guile in the wide, bright blue eyes.

When Henrik ran away, the flex of the muscles in his ass almost undid Marco completely. He came uncomfortably close to dropping to his knees in pure worship before he remembered himself. He cleared his throat. "Is, um… Is he okay? I really didn't mean to scare him off."

"He'll be all right." Gus sighed, looking guilty. "I might as well tell you. Rikky—Henrik, that is—is agoraphobic. He hasn't left our property in almost eight years."

Marco blinked, stunned into silence. It didn't take a lot of mental math to figure out that Henrik had probably spent most of his adult life in this house and the surrounding grounds. Even if he looked young for his age, he couldn't possibly be older than Marco, in his early thirties. Marco guessed he was a good bit younger than that.

He must be incredibly lonely.

The thought of it made Marco want to follow the other man, though he wasn't entirely sure what he'd do if he caught up with him. All Marco knew was, the urge to help—somehow—swelled inside him until his chest felt hot and tight with the pressure of it.

"I hope…I mean…" Marco rubbed the back of his neck, his worst nervous habit. "Fucking shit. Are you sure I didn't, like, really scare him? I mean, he looked…" He couldn't find the right words to describe the strange brew of shame, terror and palpable longing raw as an open wound on Henrik's face when he'd run away, but Gus seemed to understand. Her lips curved into a sad smile.

"I know. Trust me, though, that's not your fault. It's on me. Rikky and I grew up together. I've known him all my life, and I should've known something like this might happen." She glanced around the kitchen. "Sit down, please. I'll make some more coffee and you can tell me your thoughts about the new dining room fixture." She gave Marco's arm a comforting squeeze. "I'll talk to Rikky later, after he's had some time alone."

Nodding, Marco went to the small, round table on the far side of the breakfast bar from the large, airy kitchen. As he settled himself into a chair beside the bay window looking out on the mountains, Gus took a plastic travel mug from the counter and put it in the freezer.

§ § §

"Rikky? Wake up, honey."

Henrik jerked awake at the sound of Gus's voice. He sat up, rubbing his eyes. Gus was perched on the edge of his bed, a tall glass of iced coffee in her hand. He blinked at her. "What're you doing?"

"Bringing you your coffee." She held it out to him.

He took it and sipped. It was good, of course. Gus knew exactly the way he liked it. "Thanks."

"Sure." She chewed on her bottom lip. "Look, I'm really sorry about what happened."

He laughed. "No, you're not."

To her credit, she didn't bother to pretend anymore. She hunched her shoulders and looked guilty. He'd had time to think it over in between his post-orgasm meltdown and falling asleep—still covered in sweat and semen, he noted with distaste—and he'd realized pretty quickly that Gus had to have realized all along things would've probably played out exactly the way they did. Which made him not exactly sure how to feel right now.

Kicking aside the pillows he'd somehow gotten tangled around his legs, Henrik scooted to the other side of the bed and stood. "I need a shower. I'm sure you have other things to do."

"Marco's taking pictures and measurements in the dining room. I'm staying out of his way." Gus sighed. "Rikky, come on. You can't just sit in this house alone for the rest of your life."

"It's my life. I'll do what I want with it."

A familiar, stubborn crease dug between her eyes. He turned his back on her and went to his dresser, pretending to look for clothes they both knew he wasn't going to wear.

"You *aren't* doing anything, though. That's the thing."

She was right, of course, which just made the words cut deeper. He yanked a pair of jeans he hadn't worn in at least a year from his drawer and ignored her.

Behind him, his handmade comforter shifted with a soft whisper, then Gus's ever-present heels clicked across his wood floor. She stopped short of touching him, because she was smart that way, but she stood close enough for him to feel her presence. "You can ignore me all you want, but you know I'm right, and I *know* you know it. I love you too much to let you waste away here when we both know you need more than that."

A sudden surge of fury spun Henrik around to face his cousin, both fists tight at his side. Gus actually took a step backward, but Henrik was too angry to stop the words from coming out. "And who the hell ever said you get decide *anything* about *my* life, huh? Who put you in charge? Who the *fuck* said you get to *do* crap like this?" He shut his eyes and buried both hands in his hair, trying to unsee the way Gus backed away from him, her expression cautious. "What made you think anything was going to happen, anyway?"

"You're attracted to him." Her voice held no uncertainty, and he couldn't very well say anything since she was right. "And he's attracted to you, too. My God, Rikky, you saw how he looked at you."

His anger gone, he dropped his hands, opened his eyes and looked at her. She was quite sincere. Shaking his head, he turned back to the dresser to find a T-shirt, more for something to keep himself busy than any other reason. "So what? Do you honestly think he'd hang around and deal with all my issues once he'd gotten me into bed? Even I'm not *that* naive, Gus. I know *you're* not."

"It doesn't have to be that way. You should give him a chance."

He laughed, and it sounded as bitter as he felt in some of his darker moments. "Look, I realize you're trying to help, okay? I see that. Are you looking for forgiveness here? Because you have it." Fishing an old Mount LeConte T-shirt his grandfather had given him out of his drawer, he turned to face Gus's unhappy frown. "You're the one and only important person in my life, and I love you more than I can tell you. Of course I forgive you. But, Gus, you have to realize that no man is ever going to want me. I mean, yeah, maybe they would want to screw me. But no sane man is going to willingly put up with my problems. You have to face that. I have, ages ago." He laid the T-shirt on top of his dresser and reached for Gus's hand. "It's okay, you know. I'm all right."

She shook off his grip and backed out of reach, her arms crossed over her chest and tears glittering in her eyes. He stared, shocked. Gus never cried. Never. She was the strongest person he could imagine existing. He hadn't seen her cry since her mother died when she was nine.

Guilt squirmed in the pit of his stomach, though he couldn't have said why on a bet. "Gus, what—"

"Shut up." She wiped at her eyes, leaving a smear of mascara that threw him off even worse since she never allowed herself to look less than one hundred percent put together around anyone but Henrik. Or one of her Lances, on the morning after. "God, you just…" She flung both hands up in clear frustration. "I love you so much it hurts me sometimes. And I can't stand to see you alone. But it's even worse to watch you resigning yourself to being alone forever, and being *okay* with that."

He had no idea what to say, or how to feel. He reached behind him to lean against his dresser, because the urge to go to Gus and hold her tight was almost overwhelming and he didn't think she'd welcome it right now. "I—"

"Shut *up*." She sniffed. Wiped her eyes again and flipped a lock of hair out of her face. Her expression flowed between anger, hurt, frustration and the determination Henrik so admired about her. "Maybe you've given up on yourself. But I'll never give up on you. Not as long as I live. And you'll just have to deal with it."

On that note, she spun and stalked out of his room, slamming the door behind her. Henrik slumped against the dresser. He and Gus didn't fight often, but when they did, it inevitably left him exhausted.

He didn't really know how to feel. In a way, he knew Gus was right. He'd given up on himself. He'd resigned himself to a life alone, even though he knew he'd always want more.

On the other hand, who was Gus to question his decision in that area? He understood why it didn't sit well with her. She loved him and wanted him to be happy. Hell, he'd feel the same way if their situations were reversed. He might even try to pull something similar, though he doubted he'd be able to manage it.

He couldn't deny that he wanted happiness for himself. He wanted to fall in love, to find someone who would love him in return. But he had to be realistic. It wasn't going to happen. He'd tried to cure his disease in the past, and it hadn't worked. He wasn't enough of a starry-eyed romantic to believe the love of a good man could fix him when more conventional therapies had failed. And he sure as hell wasn't inclined to believe that just because a man wanted him meant that man would be willing to love him, as damaged as he was.

Which wasn't to say he would allow Gus to think he didn't appreciate the effort. As he'd told her, she was the single most important person in his life, and he'd do anything to make sure she knew that.

Gathering his jeans, T-shirt and a pair of underwear, he headed to the bathroom for a shower. Maybe by the time he got out, he'd feel up to facing Marco Ravél again.

Chapter Four

Marco snapped another photo of the dining room from the butler's pantry door. It was a wider shot than either of the last four he'd gotten, so maybe it wasn't a total waste of time.

He glanced over his shoulder. No sign of Augustina. She'd gone to check on her cousin at least twenty minutes ago. He knew he ought to be more patient, all things considered, but damn. Being left alone here made him uncomfortable.

Sighing, he crossed to the tall windows at the other end of the room and peered out at the lush green lawn and colorful flower beds in the front of the house. Mountain laurels lined the drive winding up the hillock on which the house sat, their branches covered with pink blossoms. The house faced west, toward the mountain, and its peak loomed green and tantalizing overhead. It was an unusual way to build. Marco wondered what the eastern view was like, down the mountain in the rear of the house. It must be stunning.

"Oh. Um…"

Henrik.

Marco turned, trying to move before the other man could run away again without moving fast enough to *make* him run away. Henrik hovered in the doorway, wearing a T-shirt that had probably been yellow once upon a time and a pair of jeans faded near-white. A hole gaped in the left knee, showing a tantalizing glimpse of thigh. His feet were bare, his hair wet and curling into fine wisps on the ends.

If he'd had a spoon Marco would've dug right in.

He smiled, hoping he didn't look quite as lecherous as he felt. "Hi." The wary look in Henrik's eyes stopped Marco from asking if he was all right.

"Hi." Henrik returned Marco's smile, still cautious but with an encouraging warmth. "I, um…I was looking for Gus. Um.

Augustina."

Okay, that wasn't exactly what Marco had expected to hear. He set his camera on the table. "I thought she was with you."

"No. She left when I went to take a shower. I thought she'd be in here." Henrik glanced over his shoulder, running one hand self-consciously through his hair. "Huh."

"Hm. Maybe…" Marco thought about it, and laughed. "Hell, I have no idea. It's not like she could've just gone down the road to the store, could she?"

Henrik looked startled, then flashed a grin that made Marco want to molest him. "No, I guess not." He shifted from one foot to the other, glanced behind him again, then faced Marco with a level of determination Marco would've thought excessive if Augustina—*Gus*, that was cute—hadn't told him about Henrik's problem. "So. Marco. I wanted to tell you how much I love your vase."

Pleased, Marco smiled. "Thank you. Gotta say, I was pretty proud of that one." He eased closer, and let his smile warm when Henrik didn't seem inclined to run. "It's *your* vase now, though. I hope you're enjoying it."

"I am. I have an arrangement of mountain laurel blossoms in it right now." Henrik rubbed his palms on his thighs and took a cautious step closer to Marco. "What do you think about the dining room? The new light fixture, I mean. Do you have any ideas?" The startlingly blue eyes widened. "Oh, I haven't thanked you yet for taking this commission. You have no idea how much I appreciate it." He gestured at the chandelier. "This thing has needed replacing for pretty much my whole life."

Marco laughed. "Hell, I should be thanking *you*. I could use the money." He glanced around him, admiring the room for the umpteenth time. "Besides, I'm looking forward to this project. This room is beautiful. Designing a light fixture for it is going to be really exciting."

There went the sweet, sunny smile again. God, Marco was going to have a hell of a time keeping his hands to himself if

Henrik kept up with this whole innocently-sexy thing. Which he no doubt would, since he obviously didn't know he was doing it.

Marco stuck his hands in the back pockets of his jeans. "To answer your question, yeah, I have some ideas. I'm thinking we should go more modern. Something that'll balance and enhance the traditional style of the room without getting lost in it, you know?"

"Yes. I think I see what you mean." Henrik began a slow circle around the table, studying the current chandelier with interest. "This one's too *fussy*, isn't it? The fake candles and gold tone don't belong in this room. It needs something more natural. More organic."

"Exactly." Marco watched Henrik's face, impressed with his insight. "You have a really sharp artistic eye, you know that?"

Henrik blushed.

"Thanks." He eyed Marco from the other side of the table, his expression suggesting intense personal struggle. "You should stay. For lunch. Have lunch with Gus and me."

Surprised, Marco stared. "What?"

The blush, which had begun to fade, came back with a vengeance, coloring Henrik's pale cheeks a deep red. He hunched his shoulders. "You probably have other things to do. I shouldn't have—" His teeth dug into his bottom lip. "Sorry." Before Marco could process what was going on, Henrik strode toward the butler's pantry door.

Oh, hell no. You are not *running away from me again.*

Marco sprang after him. "Henrik, wait." He touched Henrik's shoulder.

Henrik whirled around. His gaze locked with Marco's. This close, Marco could hear the other man's quick breaths and see the barely visible tremor in his hands. It hit Marco like a rock to the head that Henrik was holding a panic attack at bay by sheer force of will.

Marco took a step back, giving Henrik the space he needed. "I'd love to stay for lunch, if that's still okay." He peered into Henrik's eyes—those eyes that didn't seem able to hide anything—and decided to speak his mind. Or, well, part of it. "You surprised me when you asked me to stay, but I'm really glad you did. I'd like to get to know you better. I hope that's not being too forward," he added when Henrik's mouth fell open, "but you seem like a guy who appreciates honesty. So I'm just being honest."

Henrik studied him with undisguised suspicion. Marco's knees wobbled. The way Henrik's face betrayed his every thought and feeling made Marco's heart race like a prize greyhound. Which was weird, maybe, but he'd had one too many lovers who liked to play mind games. A man who didn't know *how* was rare enough that Marco found it incredibly attractive on multiple levels. He favored Henrik with his brightest smile.

Henrik laughed and shook his head. A lock of baby-fine blond hair fell across his eye. He brushed it away, which was a good thing because Marco thought he might've had to do it himself if Henrik hadn't. "Okay. Well, as long as you're being honest, I guess I can't very well do any less than that." He peered at Marco with an odd but compelling mix of amusement, shyness and desire. "I'd kind of like to get to know you better too. I'm sure Gus told you I don't exactly get out much. I love her, but it'd be nice to have someone else to talk to, even for a little while."

Standing close enough to touch the man he wanted like he hadn't wanted anyone in years, close enough to smell his shampoo and old clothes, Marco knew in his gut that a little while wasn't going to cut it. Not for him.

Kind of scary, that.

§ § §

Henrik woke just as the sun rose on Monday, ran in the cool, foggy silence of the forest for nearly an hour, then went to the gym and lifted weights until his body ran with sweat and his arms shook. Even so, he still felt restless.

He stripped and climbed into the gym's shower, hoping the pounding of the hot water would settle his mind. He'd felt nervous and twitchy ever since the day before. The day he'd spent with Marco.

To be fair, it hadn't been the whole day. Marco was a busy man, with a shop to run and art to produce. But he'd stayed for lunch, and another hour or so besides, just talking. Henrik had enjoyed himself so much he'd almost resented Gus's eventual return from the grounds, where she'd evidently gone walking to "get some fresh air and do some thinking"—meaning she'd wanted Henrik and Marco to have some time alone.

After Marco left, Henrik had floated on air for a while before his brain engaged and he began to wonder what might happen between him and Marco. He knew well enough what Marco *wanted.* Maybe he'd spent his life hidden away in this house, but he wasn't stupid. And he couldn't pretend he didn't want it too. After all, he'd gotten himself off pretending his butt plug was Marco's cock before they'd even had a proper conversation.

Sex toys weren't people, though, and Henrik wasn't naive enough to believe that real sex was remotely like the fevered fantasies he conjured in his head when he masturbated. Even watching porn online couldn't possibly prepare him for the reality of actual sex with a living, breathing man.

Closing his eyes, he leaned his head back into the water to rinse the shampoo from his hair. God. To have sex, *finally…* He wanted it—*ached* for it, so much that sometimes he had to stand still and just breathe for a while so he didn't start breaking things—but at the same time the whole idea terrified him.

More frightening, however, was the thought of Marco learning Henrik's secret. If the pain of being penetrated didn't kill him, the shame of Marco finding out he was a virgin certainly would.

Do you really think he hasn't figured it out?

Opening his eyes again, Henrik turned and switched off the shower. He wiped the water from his face. Yes, Marco most likely *had* considered the possibility that Henrik lacked experience.

Of course he had, now that Henrik thought of it. Marco was

a man of the world. Handsome, outgoing, and talented, with a keen intelligence to boot. No doubt he'd picked up on Henrik's innocence right away.

"But he still wants me," Henrik whispered to the earth-toned tiles. "Why?"

He didn't understand it. But he'd take it anyway. Life was unlikely to throw another chance like this his way, and he wasn't about to waste it. No matter how much it scared him.

§ § §

Not long after breakfast, Carl called Gus with a company emergency. Apparently the entire business was in danger of folding unless she and the VPs could fix the problem five minutes ago.

"It's just Carl being paranoid," Gus assured Henrik as she dressed for a video conference while he sat cross-legged on her bedroom floor and worried. "Every time the price of chromite drops on the world markets, even a little bit, he panics."

"Hm." Henrik chewed on his thumbnail and watched Gus slip into the blood-red heels that matched her suit. "So you don't think we're going to go under?"

"Absolutely not." Smiling, she crossed to where he sat naked on her floor and ruffled his hair. "Don't worry, Rikky. We'll be fine. I promise."

Henrik nodded, returned her smile and pushed the concern over the business out of his mind. Gus was the only one in his family who'd never tried to shelter him from the truth. She was the only person he'd ever known who'd never lied to him. If she said everything was fine, he believed her.

She sure as hell knew more about the business of mineral trading than he did. In fact, he'd long suspected she knew more about it than his father had, or his grandfather, who'd started the business in the first place. Which would explain why the old man and his shadow of a wife had retired to Vienna and left him in charge of things when his parents were killed. They never would've done it if they hadn't known for a fact that Gus would be the real power behind the throne, so to speak.

Grandpa Otto would never have given his business to a woman on paper, but he was too much of a businessman at heart to let a screw-up like Henrik actually run the multi-million dollar corporation he'd built from scratch. He'd known Gus would be the one actually running things.

Henrik had always thought he should feel disappointed by his grandfather's lack of faith in him. Instead, he'd felt nothing but relief. Gus got to do what she was born for, and he himself was spared the agony of trying and failing at something he'd never wanted to start with.

After Gus finished getting ready, Henrik followed her from her suite to the meeting room they'd created out of an unused space on the third floor. He stopped well short of the entrance, because the last thing either of them needed was for the VPs to catch a glimpse of Schweitzer International's nominal owner standing naked in the hallway. He took Gus's hands in his. "Good luck with the meeting."

"Thanks." She pecked him on the cheek and gave his fingers a squeeze before letting go. "This is likely to take a while. I'm sure I'll have to talk the guys out of closing plants again."

Henrik laughed. "Probably. And I know you can do it."

She grinned. "I'll see you when the crisis is over."

Henrik waited until Gus shut the thick wooden double doors behind her, then went to find something to occupy himself.

Unfortunately, his usual tricks didn't cut it this time. Books, cleaning and cooking did nothing to keep his mind from running in dangerous Marco-centered circles. Even a second run in the forest didn't help. No matter how fast he ran, he couldn't escape his own thoughts. The attempt left him frustrated and tired.

Eventually, his nervous energy drove him up to the attic, where he and Gus had stored all their childhood memorabilia. He took a bottle of chardonnay with him, because nothing else had worked to make him stop thinking about Marco and sex, and while wallowing in nostalgia might just do it, he knew from experience he'd need liquid courage to face his past.

Not because it was a bad or painful one. In fact, growing up here with Gus had been idyllic. He'd been diagnosed with agoraphobia in his early teens, but he'd never gotten out much on account of the remoteness of the estate, so he'd always been able to brush off the seriousness of his disease. Until the first time he'd tried to go into town with Gus, to celebrate her eighteenth birthday, and come face to face with the reality of it.

He'd tried, over and over again. Tried facing his fears, tried psychiatrists and meds, tried meditation and all kinds of other treatments. When he'd finally admitted to himself that he couldn't be cured and he would never leave this estate again, he'd hidden all memories of his glorious growing-up years in the attic and moved from his old room to the former guest suite on the first floor.

He took a long swallow from the wine bottle—already a third empty—before opening the attic door and walking inside. Dust, stirred by his passage, swirled in the sunlight spilling through the arched window tucked under the eave on the other end of the room. As he went he ran his free hand over the top of a short freestanding shelf piled with books, leaving finger trails in the dust.

He sneezed. Sneezed again. He rubbed his nose and wiped his watery eyes. A loose floorboard caught at his foot. He stumbled, felt a sharp pain in the ball of his foot and set the wine bottle on a pile of boxes so he could take out the splinter lodged in the soft spot between calluses.

Stupid splinter. He flicked it into a darkened corner, picked up his wine and resumed his perusal of the space around him. Turning in a slow circle, he studied the piles of books, clothes, boxes, toys and other things. Smiling, he took another swig from the bottle. He used to love to play up here as a kid. He and Gus used to play haunted house here on rainy days. They'd even camped out in here sometimes. Those long-ago nights in the attic, lying in sleeping bags and whispering together long after midnight, he and Gus had talked about the things they'd do when they were grown. They'd travel the world—together, of course. They'd be famous adventurers. Climb the highest mountains, conquer the ocean's deepest trenches, penetrate the last of the planet's unexplored jungles and gain the trust of primitive people who'd never before had contact with the outside world. They'd become the toast of high society. They'd go to fancy parties, drink expensive champagne and eat caviar and laugh at all the snobby people there.

That was before Henrik had been forced to face the reality of his future. He'd accepted it, eventually. But it hadn't been easy, and God, it *hurt* to come up here and remember those days when he'd believed the whole world to be his for the taking.

So don't do it.

Rolling his eyes, he put the bottle to his lips again and drank a long swallow. "Shut up," he told the voice in his head. It was far too sensible for his liking, especially at times like these, when he felt a need to hurt himself on purpose in order to get rid of worse things than his memories.

After all, what could possibly be more painful than a promise just within reach that he knew damn well could never be fulfilled?

The fact that he was definitely going to take whatever Marco would give him, for however long he could have it, just made the whole mess worse. The only way he knew of to not think about it for a while was to think of something else. And apparently nothing but his past had a prayer of displacing Marco in his brain.

He stopped to stare at himself in the old mirror propped on top of a box of encyclopedias. "You're an idiot." He pointed at his dim, wavy reflection with the hand holding the wine bottle. "Look at you. Naked and halfway drunk in the fucking attic, trying to make yourself maudlin on purpose so you won't go nuts thinking about losing your virginity at *twenty-seven years old*." He laughed, shaking his head. "It's pathetic, is what it is."

Head whirling from wine and confusion, he turned away from the mirror and made his way through the maze of furniture and boxes to the blanket-covered pile under the window. He stared at it for a moment, his pulse thudding at the base of his throat. He took another healthy drink. Kicked at the pile with one bare foot.

A small framed photo tumbled out from beneath the blanket. He peered down at it. Through the years of dust and dirt coating the glass, he saw himself and Gus dressed as pirates, both holding their plastic swords high above their heads, their expressions fierce. They looked ready to conquer the universe.

In a burst of insight, Henrik knew this wouldn't work. The dashed hopes of his past and the false hope that Marco represented in the here and now surrounded him, pulled on him from opposite directions, and left him no safe place to turn.

A familiar burgeoning panic clawed at the inside of his chest. Throat tight and eyes burning, he stumbled to the door and down to the safety of the third floor hallway.

Shaking, he slid down the wall to sit on the floor and drank until the wine numbed the fear and self-hate eating at his insides.

By the time Henrik climbed to his feet and staggered back downstairs, he'd finished the bottle and decided he needed another one. Gus was still in her meeting. He heard the raised voices of some of the veeps and Gus's calm one as he passed. He wondered what the men would say if he busted in, bare-assed and shitfaced, carrying an empty wine bottle, but he figured Gus would be mad and he didn't want that, even if it would've been funny as hell to see the shocked faces on the video screens.

He managed to get to the kitchen without incident, in spite of the way the floor moved. He deposited the bottle in the recycling container and headed toward the fridge. They had a decent bottle of zinfandel in there, if he remembered right.

Something went *bing-bong*. He frowned. What the hell?

It took him a second to remember that sound was the front doorbell. He laughed. No one used their *doorbell*. Who ever came out here?

Maybe it was someone selling Girl Scout cookies. Gus had brought home some of those once. They were *awesome*. Stomach rumbling at the thought, Henrik strode toward the front of the house.

The bell sounded again before he got there. Irritated, he yelled, "Hold your horses, I'm coming!"

Trotting the last few feet to the front door, he took hold of the knob, turned it and flung open the door.

It wasn't the Girl Scouts.

Marco Ravél grinned at him. "We have *got* to stop meeting like this."

Maybe it was the wine. Maybe it was the worries and daydreams chasing each other around his brain all day. Maybe a little of both. Whatever the reason, Henrik didn't even try to stop himself from flinging his arms around Marco's neck and taking the kiss he'd been dreaming of for days.

Chapter Five

Shocked into immobility, Marco stood there for a couple of eternal seconds and let Henrik kiss him. He couldn't blink, couldn't even draw a breath, because Henrik's lips were pressed to his, Henrik's body molded to his, and fucking *hell* the man was naked again. *Why* did he have to be naked?

Marco managed to make his arms move, the intent being to pull Henrik off him. All this was happening too fast. Something felt off, and Marco intended to find out what it was before his brain stopped working and the two of them ended up doing something Henrik would most likely regret later. Then Henrik's tongue swiped at Marco's lips, and he forgot about everything else.

Wrapping one arm snug around Henrik's waist, Marco buried the other hand in Henrik's soft blond hair and angled his head to kiss him deep. Henrik opened to Marco with a low sound of surrender that set a hot glow in Marco's belly. Heart galloping a mile a minute, he tightened his arm around Henrik and let himself sink into the wet warmth of Henrik's mouth on his.

The second his tongue found Henrik's, the wrongness Marco sensed before came into sharp focus. Henrik's clumsy eagerness plus the tang of wine on his breath made it obvious.

Marco forced himself to unwind his arm from Henrik's body, let go of his hair and grasp his shoulders. It wasn't easy, but he couldn't let himself take this any further when Henrik was not only drunk, but even more inexperienced than Marco had thought.

He pushed Henrik away, gently but firmly. It took more strength than he'd imagined. Henrik might not be bulky, but his body was solid muscle, and he was dead set on not letting go in this lifetime.

Finally, Henrik dropped his arms from around Marco's neck and stood staring at him with a heart-melting combination of longing and confusion. "What? Marco? I thought you wanted me."

"I do." *God, you have no idea how much.* Marco glanced from Henrik's wide blue eyes to his kiss-reddened lips and back up again, holding Henrik's gaze with grim determination. The last thing he needed was to give in to the temptation to get an eyeful of Henrik's goods. He laid a hand on Henrik's flushed cheek. "This isn't the right time, Henrik. You'll regret it."

Henrik's brow furrowed, making him look remarkably like Gus for a second. "Don't tell me how I feel. You don't know."

Marco licked his lips. How wrong was it that he found Angry Henrik even *more* attractive? Christ.

"Of course not. But…" Marco fumbled for the right words to tell Henrik he knew his secret, but nothing appropriately gentle came to mind. Watching Henrik's expression turn thunderous and wondering if he was about to get punched in the face, Marco decided to just go with the bare truth. "Look, I know you've never… Well, done any of this before."

To his dismay, Henrik went dead white and broke away from Marco's grip. He turned away, looking stricken. "Go away."

"What? No, wait!"

Marco lunged and grabbed Henrik's arm just in time to stop him from running inside and slamming the door behind him. Henrik fought to break free, but his efforts were hampered by his apparent determination to keep his head down and his face hidden. Marco got his arms around Henrik's chest and held him tight, his back to Marco's front and his arms tense at his sides. His head hung forward, his face still hidden beneath his hair. Fine tremors ran through his body, and his breath came fast and short.

Marco planted a tender kiss on the back of Henrik's neck, because he couldn't help himself. "Don't be like that. It's okay. You hear me? It's okay." He nuzzled behind Henrik's ear. Easing one hand from around Henrik's upper body, he raked the fine blond strands away from Henrik's face. "I still want you. Just as much as before. Okay?"

Henrik raised his head, turned and peered at Marco. The hope and fear in his eyes told Marco he'd nailed Henrik's insecurities dead center. "You do?"

"Yeah. I do." Marco raked his fingers through Henrik's hair again. He loved the way the silky strands slid over his skin. "Have you *seen* yourself? Come on, man."

A faint smile turned up the corners of Henrik's mouth. He didn't say anything, but his body went from rigid to halfway relaxed in Marco's embrace.

Marco rested his cheek against Henrik's head, so he wouldn't have to look Henrik in the eye when he said the uncomfortably self-revealing next words. "You're not just some random guy. And I can't take you to bed when I know you're not really in the right headspace for it yet."

Henrik drew a deep, shaking breath and let it out. One hand came up to clutch Marco's wrist. "I want a man to fuck me." The words emerged in a rough, trembling whisper. "I've wanted it for a long time. I never thought it would happen, then…" His fingers dug into Marco's flesh until Marco grimaced. "I know we just met each other, but I might never have another chance like this, and…well…I want it to be you."

The unspoken question came through as clearly as if Henrik had shouted. A peculiar feeling squirmed in Marco's chest. Clutching Henrik to him as tight as he could, he kissed the pale cheek beside his. "It will be. Another day, when you're sober, and you're really ready."

This time, Henrik's smile shone with relief. God, he was beautiful. Everything he felt was right there on his face for the world to see. Marco had always had a thing for honest men, and he'd eat his fucking shoes if Henrik was even capable of dishonesty. It made him irresistible, even if he hadn't been one of the most physically gorgeous men Marco had ever laid eyes on.

Which he was.

Fuck. Marco had to get Henrik inside and dressed before his

good sense got knocked sideways and he took the man right here on the front stoop.

He cleared his throat. "Henrik? Why don't we go inside now? I'll make you something to eat and we can talk about the new dining room light."

Henrik turned and studied him for a long, nerve-wracking moment before nodding. "Okay." He took Marco's hand and wove their fingers together, his stare bold. "Is that why you came over here? To discuss the fixture?"

The lilt in his voice and the curve of his lips said he knew better. Marco didn't see any good reason to pretend otherwise, especially now. He grinned. "That was my excuse."

Henrik laughed. It was a wonderful sound. One Marco wanted to hear more of it.

Following Henrik into the house, Marco promised himself he would.

§ § §

"Well, this is a pleasant surprise."

Marco jumped. He'd completely forgotten about Gus.

Straightening up, he turned around to smile at her where she stood in the butler's pantry doorway, an amused look on her face. "Hi. Sorry I didn't call first, I just got the urge to come over, and… uh…"

"Look at his design, Gus!" Hurrying forward, Henrik—who'd put on clothes after he and Marco had come inside, thank God—grabbed his cousin's hand and dragged her toward the dining room table. He swept his free hand toward the giant pad of paper he'd dug out of Gus's office supplies, on which Marco had drawn up his ideas for the new light fixture. "It's going to be absolutely amazing."

Gus shook loose of Henrik's grip and pinned him with a stern glare. "How much've you had to drink?"

"None of your business." He met her disapproving gaze with a mild but unyielding stare.

Marco kept quiet. Whatever the subtext here, it was sure as shit none of *his* business.

The cousins glowered at one another for several seconds that felt more like years to Marco, who doodled on the edge of the paper with the pencil and pretended not to notice the silent battle going on a couple feet away.

Finally, Gus sighed and turned away from Henrik to study the drawings Marco had done. Her eyebrows rose. She looked up at Marco. "This is perfect. Exactly what this room needs."

He smiled, pleased that she liked his vision for the light and relieved she and Henrik had stopped quiet-fighting. He hated when people did that, especially when he had no clue what was going on. "Thanks." He tapped one finger on the top of the design. "This part's going to be custom-made wrought iron, to match your drapery rods. I have a friend in town who's a blacksmith. She's already said she'll do this part. She's one of the few people I know who can handle iron work that delicate."

"The rest of it is hand-blown glass." Shoving his way between Gus and Marco, Henrik ran a fingertip over the network of glass beads hanging from the simple iron framework in the sketch. "He's going to have cloudy beads strung close together in the frame to cover the globe and diffuse the light. The rest of the beads hang down so they look like raindrops." He raised his head and glanced from Gus to Marco and back again, grinning ear to ear. "It's beautiful, isn't it?"

"Yes. It really is." Gus squeezed Marco's shoulder. "I can hardly wait to see the real thing."

"Hopefully you'll be able to see it sooner rather than later. I'm planning to start on the beads tomorrow." Marco sought Henrik's gaze, caught and held it. Instantly, his pulse picked up and his knees wobbled. Damn. He could get addicted to the way Henrik laser-stared straight into his brain. "I may not be able to come back up the mountain for a few days, what with running the shop and working on the light and other stuff. But you can call my cell anytime you need me. For anything."

Henrik's cheeks pinked and his eyes went hot. Gus mouthed a silent *oh* and shot a sly sideways glance at Henrik. Marco grinned, knowing he looked like he was thinking exactly what he was thinking and not giving a goddamn. Gus had played matchmaker here. She ought to be tickled that her efforts had been such a success.

She clicked her nails on the back of a chair. "So you guys exchanged numbers, huh?"

Henrik went even redder. "Um…"

"Of course." Marco gave Gus his best innocent look. "What if I have a new idea I need to run by him? Or he has one he'd like to tell me? We need to be able to contact each other."

"Right." She glanced between the two of them with a smug smirk she didn't even try to hide. "Well. Enjoy *discussing your ideas*." She put air quotes around the final phrase, which made Marco snicker and Henrik groan and cover his face. "Rikky, I'm changing clothes and going into town for a while."

He lifted his head and frowned at her. "Is everything okay? Didn't the meeting go well?"

Meeting? Marco watched Gus and Henrik both with undisguised curiosity. Maybe one of them would tell him what that meant.

Or not. Gus shrugged without paying any attention to Marco. "It went all right. Some of the veeps are still a little nervous, but I got Carl under control. He'll settle everyone else down."

Henrik scratched his elbow. "I didn't think you had business in town today. And we still have plenty of supplies. We just got a delivery the other day."

Marco resisted the urge to nod to himself. He'd been wondering how Henrik and Gus managed grocery shopping way up here, an hour from anything resembling civilization. He should've thought of a delivery service. Even people who *weren't* filthy rich used them these days.

Gus shook her head. "No, you're right. There's nothing we

need. I guess I'm just feeling restless. I'd like to get out."

"Oh." With a quick glance at Marco, Henrik turned to face Gus and touched her arm. "Are you okay?"

It didn't take much brain power to figure out that Gus probably didn't just take off for town without a goal in mind unless she felt troubled for some reason. Not wanting to intrude on anything private, Marco moved away, pretending to study the ceiling. He couldn't help catching a glimpse of Gus's face, though, and she didn't look upset or anything. In fact, she looked like a woman headed for a hook up, or at least in the market for one.

"I'm fine. Honest." Gus took Henrik's hand and kissed him on the cheek. When his eyes narrowed in obvious disbelief, she laughed. "Rikky, come on. Everything's *fine*, I promise. I just feel like going to town, that's all."

"Okay." Henrik still radiated suspicion and worry, but he didn't say anything. He pulled Gus into a hug. "Have fun, and be careful."

"Always. Love you."

"Love you too."

She squeezed her cousin tight, then let him go and stepped back. "If I'm not going to be home tonight, I'll text you." She strode back toward the kitchen, heading for the garage entrance. "Nice to see you, Marco."

"Yeah, you too." He waved at her. After she'd gone, he raised his eyebrows at Henrik. "What's that all about?"

Henrik shot him a look suggesting he'd gone off his meds. "She's young, rich, unattached and drop-dead gorgeous. What do *you* think?"

Okay, so Henrik wasn't *that* innocent. Marco laughed. "I get you. Well, good for her."

"Yeah." With a deep sigh, Henrik leaned his butt against the table. "I hope there won't be a Lance this time."

"Um. Okay." Since Henrik didn't seem inclined to explain, Marco didn't ask. "So…"

"Shut up."

Marco shut up, more from surprise than anything else. He watched with continued astonishment and growing need as Henrik approached him, eyes bright with determination and body in full-on slink mode. Marco surveyed Henrik from his tousled hair to his bare feet and every perfectly formed inch in between. He wore the same ratty jeans and threadbare T-shirt he'd had on the day before. Why in the name of all things holy and not was that *so* fucking sexy?

"Ohmygod," Marco breathed when Henrik pressed close enough for him to smell wine, dust and a faint spice of sweat. "Hen—"

"Shhhh." Henrik slipped an arm around Marco's waist. Marco shushed, because damned if he could've made a sound right then even if a busload of orphans depended on it. Henrik smiled, slow and seductive. "Kiss me."

Alarm bells clanged in Marco's head. "Wh… I… uh…"

"It won't go any further than that. I promise. But I know you can't stay much longer, and you won't be back for who knows how long." Henrik gazed at Marco with a look he couldn't begin to decipher—lust, loneliness, a lingering hint of fear, and a whole giant tangle of more complex things swirling under the surface. He touched Marco's pierced eyebrow, moving the tiny silver ring with his thumb. "Just one kiss. Please."

Marco wanted to say the problem lay with him, not Henrik. That he wasn't sure he could stop with one kiss, especially if Henrik decided to push the issue after all. Since his power of speech apparently hadn't recovered, however, Marco decided he might as well give Henrik what he wanted.

This time, without the shock factor involved, Marco was free to enjoy every second of it. He shut his eyes and let himself savor the enthusiastic press of Henrik's tongue, his sweet little pleasure sounds, the warmth of his skin radiating through the thin T-shirt.

Marco tried not to notice the hardness digging into his hip.

He'd totally lose control if he did.

True to his word, Henrik didn't protest when Marco broke away. He did cling, though, both fists clutching Marco's shirt as if he'd drift away without that double grip to anchor him. He favored Marco with a dazed grin. "I really like kissing you."

Marco grinned back, as dazed as Henrik. "I really like kissing you, too." *Understatement of the fucking year.* He ran his hand through Henrik's hair, because he was already hooked on the silky slide of it between his fingers. "You're a bold man, Henrik."

Those brilliant blue eyes blinked at him. "No one's ever said that to me before."

"I'm gonna go out on a limb here and say that's probably because you don't normally meet people at the door naked, throw yourself into their arms and kiss them before they can even say hello." Marco silenced Henrik's laughter with another kiss, light and quick. Shit, kissing him felt way too easy. Way too comfortable. "Okay. I really should go. Darryl's alone at the shop and he doesn't like having to run the place by himself for too long."

The smile faded from Henrik's face. Leaning forward, he tucked his head into the curve of Marco's neck, both arms looped around Marco's waist. "Will you call me?"

The uncertainty in Henrik's voice made Marco want to throw the man over his shoulder, take him home and keep him naked in bed for at least a week. If it hadn't been for Henrik's agoraphobia—not to mention his virginity—he might've done it.

Good God, what in the fuck are you getting yourself into here?

He ignored the tiny voice prodding at the back of his brain. After all, they weren't exactly getting married.

"Hell yeah, I'm calling you." Marco ran a palm over the curve of Henrik's ass. The worn jeans were missing the right rear pocket, which was great as far as Marco was concerned since it meant that much less fabric between his palm and Henrik's butt. He liked that almost as much as he liked the way his touch made Henrik shiver. "I'm calling and texting every day until I get to come back here and take you to bed."

Henrik's hands gripped Marco tighter. His lips brushed Marco's neck, sending a wave of gooseflesh up his arms. Henrik lifted his head, let go of Marco and stepped back. "Okay. You'd better go then."

"Yeah. I guess so." Marco eyed Henrik from a couple of feet away. The ancient jeans did not one thing to hide the ridge of his cock. Hard as a damn teenager at a strip club.

Christ.

Marco wondered if he'd survive walking out of here without fucking that man.

You will. You got no choice.

Yeah.

He cleared his throat and did his best to smile as if he didn't want to tackle Henrik to the wide-plank hardwood floor and do perverted things to him. "All right. I'm off. I'll text you later, okay?"

"Okay." Henrik smiled, a wide, sunny smile that made Marco feel pinned to the wall. "When you come back, I'll be ready."

Oh, God.

Unable to make a single sound past the pulse thudding in his throat, Marco kept his smile in place, nodded, turned and made his way to the front door on shaky legs.

Chapter Six

Before Marco, the passage of time had never really affected Henrik much. The days had bled together, one very much like another. He hadn't minded, really. It was what it was.

Then along came an artist with a wicked smile, a gentle touch and a kiss Henrik still felt down to his marrow every time he shut his eyes. The five days since had crawled by more at the pace of centuries, in spite of the frequent calls and texts between him and Marco.

In the darkness of the small deck where he stood, gazing out over the lights of Gatlinburg far below, Henrik laid his fingertips on his lips. Marco had kissed him. *Really* kissed him. So what if he'd initiated the whole thing? Marco wouldn't have done it if he hadn't wanted to. He'd have told Henrik, nicely but in no uncertain terms, *no*.

If Henrik were truthful with himself—and he liked to think he was—that was what he found most attractive about Marco. His honesty.

Of course, the strong neck and sinewy forearms didn't hurt. Neither did the sinful curve of his mouth, or the dark eyes that stared straight into Henrik's most secret thoughts.

With a deep sigh, Henrik pushed away from the deck railing and stretched the stiffness out of his back. A cool, damp breeze brought the scent of rain. He rubbed his bare arms. He should probably go inside, but he didn't want to. Inside, he'd be able to hear Gus's party.

He understood the need for occasional investor parties, but he *hated* listening to the noise, even from a distance. It made him nervous. Locking the door to his suite didn't entirely erase the fear of some random stranger—or a group of them, more likely—stumbling drunk and half-dressed into his domain. Thus his presence here, on this little hidden deck on the far side of the cabanas surrounding the courtyard outside his suite. His grandmother had thought the people who used to stay in the guest suite would enjoy using the deck as a scenic overlook, since it boasted a stunning view of the valley. But guests—in the days when they used to stay here—mostly forgot it existed, what with the pool, hot tub, private bar and all the rest of the amenities in the courtyard and surrounding area.

Henrik, however, loved the solitude here. It was his secret spot. The place he went when the threat of the world Outside intruded on his fortress and he needed to escape.

Like now.

A chilly, restless wind rolled down off the mountain, lifted his hair and whipped it into tangles. Along with the wind came the first raindrops, stinging cold on his skin.

"Crap." Shooting a pointed glare at the sky, Henrik snatched his phone from the chair and hurried indoors.

He crossed the cabana that opened onto the deck and sprinted across the courtyard. The rain went from a light sprinkle to a steady shower just as he reached the shelter of the open-air bar on the far side. With one last, longing glance toward his secret deck, he crossed the bar area and went inside.

He'd left the recessed lighting in his sitting room ceiling on the lowest setting, giving the room a soft golden glow. He detoured to give his vase a quick caress before heading to his bedroom.

The towel he'd used earlier after his shower still hung over the back of his chair. He used it to dry himself off, tossed it back on the chair, and flopped down onto the bed.

He was looking for the TV remote when his phone rang. Startled, he leaned over and snatched it off the bedside table. He grinned when he saw Marco's picture on the display. Thumbing it on, he lay down and held the phone to his ear. "Hi, Marco."

"Hey, Rik. How's the party?"

Henrik laughed, partly because Marco knew damn well he wouldn't be anywhere near Gus's party but mostly because he *loved* how Marco had picked up Gus's nickname for him, shortened it and made it his own. "It's loud. I can hear it in my room, even though they're on the other side of the house." He pushed up on one elbow and kicked at the covers, in case he'd lost his remote in the bed. Nope. "I *was* outside where I couldn't hear, but it started raining so I had to come in, and now I can't find my TV remote."

Marco chuckled, a rich, rumbling sound that Henrik imagined would feel like worn leather, if he could touch it. "Poor Rik. How do you *live* that way?"

"Shut up, you ass." His grin still firmly in place, Henrik stretched out on the cool sheets and wished Marco was there with him. "So, what're you up to? You're not still working this late, are you? It's after eleven."

"Naw, I just laid off for the night." Something rustled on the other end of the line. Henrik pretended it was Marco's clothes coming off and falling to the floor. "All the cloudy beads are done, and I've started on the raindrop beads. I was thinking I might add a few little streaks of blue here and there. Same shade as in your vase. What d'you think?"

I think your voice could make me come all by itself. Closing his eyes, Henrik reached between his legs to cup his balls. "I think that sounds beautiful."

For a moment, he heard nothing but Marco's breathing. When Marco spoke, his words came out low and rough. "Are you touching yourself right now, Rik?"

Henrik's eyes popped open. "What? How did—?"

"Never mind." More breathing, light and quick. "Tell me. Tell me what you're doing right now."

Oh, my God. Henrik's heartbeat picked up into a gallop fast enough to make him dizzy. His cock went from half-mast to achingly stiff before he could properly process what Marco said. He swallowed. "What?"

"Tell me what you're doing. How you're getting yourself off." More rustling. Marco let out a faint, helpless moan that almost made Henrik drop the phone. "I'm so fucking hard right now, just thinking about you lying there naked, with your hand around your cock and your legs spread, jerking yourself off." Another moan, which Henrik echoed this time. "That's what I'm doing. I'm jacking my cock, thinking of you. It's hard and hot and fuck, I wish I had *your* cock in my hand instead of mine."

Henrik stared at the ceiling without seeing it. His heart pounded so hard it hurt, his breath coming short. He'd heard of phone sex, of course, but he'd never done it. Had never even imagined he'd have the chance. Yet here he was. He'd always thought it would feel silly, but it didn't. He *liked* it. He was actually going to do it.

So, might as well do it right.

"I have a toy," he heard himself whisper. His throat closed up and refused to let anything else out. Biting his lip, he rolled over to open his drawer and get out the butt plug and lube.

Marco's sharp indrawn breath told Henrik he'd said exactly the right thing. "What kind of toy?"

Henrik had to clear his throat and try twice before he got the words out, but he managed. "B-butt plug. I-I got it online." He bit his lip, then soldiered on. "I like to put it in and pretend it's you fucking me."

"Oh, shit. Thank you Jesus." Marco panted into the phone, sounding every bit as on-edge as Henrik felt. "Do it, babe. Put that plug up your ass for me. Tell me what it feels like."

Henrik could barely breathe, but he needed his toy inside him right now, and damned if he didn't *want* to tell Marco how it felt.

Flipping open the lube with one hand, he squeezed way more than he really needed into his palm, pushed the lid shut against his hip and reached between his splayed legs to smear the slippery gel around his anus. "I've got the butt plug in my hand," he said, his voice shaking, as he reached for the toy. "I'm all lubed up and ready so I can push it right in."

"You… don't need to stretch yourself first?"

"No. I just shove it in there. It's not all that big." Pulling his right leg up, Henrik aimed the plug at his hole and pushed. The tight muscles eased open to let the toy slide right in, just like always. He switched on the vibrator and let out a satisfied hum as the toy stretched him. "I'm putting it in now. It vibrates, you know. God, it feels good. I love how it opens me up. How it makes me feel full." He got the plug fully seated and twisted the base so that it grazed his gland. The sensation sparked across his nerve endings, tearing a groan from his throat. "Oh. It's gonna be so much better when it's your cock inside me, Marco."

On the other end of the line, Marco let out a low, tortured sound. "Jesus Christ, Rik. I'm so close. Let me hear you come."

The desperate growl in Marco's voice sent Henrik tumbling toward the edge himself. He arched and squirmed, one hand holding the phone to his ear and the other wrapped around his erection. Squeezing his eyes shut, he conjured an image of Marco in his mind's eye—naked, flushed, eyes closed and mouth open, those long, scarred, nimble fingers curled around his cock...

God, his cock. Long, but not *too* long, thick and dark, the head slick and shiny and a little bit red. Yes. That's what he'd look like, Henrik was sure of it. He shifted his hips enough to jar the toy inside him and pictured Marco between his legs, staring down at him with that intense, penetrating gaze while he pushed his thick, slick, perfect cock into Henrik's ass.

Henrik came with a cry he couldn't hold back. Through the haze of orgasm, he heard Marco curse and grunt. The mental picture of Marco coming sent a fresh wave of heat through Henrik's body. He moaned, thinking of the way the semen would splash onto Marco's belly, a lovely gleaming white against his dusky skin.

The moment seemed to stretch on for ages. Henrik milked his cock until it hurt, until no more fluid came out and he began to soften. Even after he finally let go of his cock and turned off the butt plug's vibrator, he left the toy inside himself. With his eyes closed, he could almost pretend Marco was there, that the butt plug was Marco's cock still inside him after they'd both come.

Maybe Marco would do that, when they had sex for real. Maybe he would lie on top of Henrik, stroke his hair and kiss him and tell him how good it was, how good they were together, all with his cock still lodged deep in Henrik's body and Henrik's legs still wound around his waist.

A pleasant shiver ran down Henrik's back, and he smiled. Soon.

"Good Lord." Marco sighed in Henrik's left ear, the sound ripe with satisfaction. "You're really something else, you know that?"

"Mmm." Peeling his eyelids open, Henrik dragged his fingers through the puddles of fluid on his belly. "That's good, right?"

Marco laughed. "Yeah, that's good." His voice dropped to the low, grumbling register Henrik liked best. "Listening to you come? That's the sexiest fucking thing I've ever heard in my life."

"It was, yes. Listening to you, I mean." Henrik rubbed his sticky palm over his heart, as if he could touch the odd, sweet warmth expanding in his chest. "I've never done anything like that before."

"I kind of figured you might not've." Marco hesitated a moment. "I'm glad you did it with me."

The strange sensation beneath Henrik's breastbone grew stronger. He dug his fingers into his pecs, unable to decide whether he liked it or not. "Me too."

Silence. After a moment, Marco let out a soft laugh. "Well. I guess we should both get some sleep. I gotta get up and get some more work done in the morning before I open the shop, and I know how much you like to get up early and run."

"Yeah." Henrik looked around his room. For the first time, it seemed as much a prison as a haven. "I wish I could be there with you."

Marco made a startled noise. "Me too. Even better, I wish I could be up there with *you*. But don't worry. It'll happen soon enough, right?"

It wouldn't. Not when Henrik wanted nothing more than to lie in Marco's arms *now*, not *soon*, whenever that might be.

He'd never felt as trapped as he did in that moment.

All of which he kept to himself. "Of course," he answered instead, hoping his voice wouldn't give him away. If Marco had been here, he would've read everything on Henrik's face. But he wasn't. And if he had been, Henrik wouldn't have had this sudden rush of bitterness to fight off anyway.

"Rik? You okay?"

Suspicion. Marco noticed everything. It warmed Henrik's heart and made him even lonelier, all at the same time.

He smiled at his own over-the-top angst. "I'm fine. Just looking forward to the day you come back up the mountain."

There. Maybe he sounded like a maiden pining away for her prince, but at least he didn't sound depressed.

"Me too." Marco's relief came through loud and clear over the phone. Good. "Well. Night, Rik. Sweet dreams."

"Night."

Henrik waited until the connection cut, then turned off his phone and set it aside. He rolled onto his side and lay staring at the wall, thinking about Marco and phone sex and what he would do right now if he could bring himself to leave the estate.

Eventually, he fell asleep with semen dried to a crust on his abdomen and his butt plug still in place, and dreamed of Marco.

§ § §

Tuesday morning, Marco was still getting distracted thinking about the sound of Rik coming.

He stopped in the middle of cleaning his shop's glass display case to remember how Rik had dropped the phone last night and keened as if he didn't care who heard, after Marco described in excruciating detail all the ways he planned to apply his tongue to Henrik's naked body.

Damn, but the man's total lack of inhibition turned Marco on like nothing else. He hadn't jerked off as much in *years* as he had in the days since Rik had first kissed him. Not just with Rik on the phone last night and Saturday night, but in the mornings when he woke up hard as iron remembering filthy scenarios shaped on the phone by Rik's soft, shy voice, or in the shower in the afternoons, washing off the sweat from the hot shop and thinking of Rik's bare body in the sunlight.

What he thought about more than anything else, though—while running the register, talking to customers, pretending to watch TV at night—was kissing Rik. Long, slow, lazy kisses, the kind where you stretched out on the grass together and did nothing else all afternoon. As much as he wanted to fuck Rik, he wanted to kiss him again even more.

When he bothered to think about it, he wondered if that wasn't kind of weird. In the past, when he'd started seeing someone new, he'd always thought of sex more than anything else.

Of course, he'd never been with anyone before who he couldn't see any time he wanted. Maybe that had something to do with it. He wasn't quite sure *what*, exactly, but the two things had to hook up somehow. Otherwise, the unexpectedly romantic turn of his fantasies just didn't make any damn sense.

"Hey! Marco. Snap out of it."

Marco jumped, dropped the paper towel he'd been using to wipe down the display case and turned to face Darryl's grin with the best blank face he could muster. "What?"

"*What*, he says." Darryl rolled his eyes. "Please. You're daydreaming again. It's almost time to open. We're not gonna be ready if we don't hustle."

Darryl was right, which annoyed the crap out of Marco. He scowled. "We'll be ready. Make sure the register's set." Picking up his paper towel, he went back to cleaning. "And I'm not daydreaming."

He got a *yeah, right* look from Darryl, but the younger man went to check the register without argument, which suited Marco just fine. He sure as hell didn't need his assistant picking on him about Rik.

Not that he *knew* about Rik, exactly. Marco hadn't told him. Hadn't told anyone, actually. He didn't want to. His friends and family would probably think he was nuts to take on a twenty-something virgin who never left the house.

He liked to think he hadn't told them because he didn't want to listen to anyone badmouth Rik—sweet, intelligent, one-of-a-kind Rik—or whatever it was developing between the two of them.

He tried not to listen to the more honest parts of himself telling him he might be just a little bit ashamed.

§ § §

The cool, cloudy weather didn't keep the tourists off the streets today. Marco and Darryl stayed busy all morning. Darryl even sold the ultra-modern six foot steel-and-obsidian sculpture that had been gathering dust in the corner, a feat Marco had started to believe impossible. He loved the piece himself, as it had been born of one of his darker moods a few months ago and in his opinion those particular creative fits resulted in some of his best work. However, he didn't kid himself that most buyers agreed with him. The sculpture tended to make people nervous, with its harsh angles and the way it seemed about to attack. Thus, its position in the back corner.

After he and Darryl had loaded the piece into the clearly delighted young couple's SUV, Marco clapped Darryl on the shoulder. "Great job, man. I was wondering if that thing was going to be shop decoration forever."

Darryl beamed. "Thanks. Gotta say, it's my favorite piece of yours. I'm kind of sorry to see it go."

Surprised, Marco smiled as the two of them headed inside. "I wouldn't've thought that was your kind of thing. You generally go for more classic styles."

"Yeah, I do, usually." Darryl shrugged, his expression thoughtful. "That sculpture just has this *energy*, you know? Almost like it's alive. All your sculpture has that vibe. Most modern stuff isn't like that. It's too cold and static. That's the difference, I guess."

Settling on the stool behind the register, Marco studied his assistant's familiar face. Brown eyes, close-cropped black hair, soft brown skin, enviable bone structure and a smile that attracted women like a ninety-percent-off shoe sale. Handsome without being intimidating about it. He looked like your friendly neighborhood college student body president, not an art critic. Who knew?

Darryl glanced down at his clothes with a frown. "What? Do I have something on me?"

"No." Marco grinned. "You have hidden depths. I like it."

"Hey. No funny business. I'm all about the ladies." Darryl pointed a warning finger, serious as a stroke except for the sparkle in his eyes.

Marco let out a deep sigh. "There you go, ripping out my poor old heart again."

The bell on the door jangled when Darryl was in mid-snicker. Marco glanced up and smiled. "Hi, Gus. How are you?" He hopped up to meet her. She'd stopped by a couple of times since that fateful first day, and he always loved seeing her.

"I'm great, Marco. How about yourself?" She strode forward, took his hands and lifted her cheek for his kiss.

"Wonderful. Business is booming today." He gave her hands a squeeze before letting go. "How's Rik?"

"He's fine. Said to tell you he misses you." She winked at him, then turned to Darryl as he strode toward her. "Well, hello, handsome."

"Hey there, beautiful." He kissed her cheek, though to Marco's eye it seemed just a hair beyond a friendly greeting. "Lovely as always to see you, Ms. Pryce."

One perfect blonde brow arched upward. "Thank you, Mr. Fields. Delightful to see you also."

She took Darryl's hand in hers. Not a strange thing, in and of itself. But the contact—skin to skin and gaze to gaze—lasted just long enough to get the gears in Marco's brain turning.

Finally, Gus let go, though Marco could've sworn she dragged her nails over Darryl's palm. She faced Marco with her all-business expression. "Marco, I'd like to buy something for myself this time."

He blinked, surprised for no reason he could pinpoint. "Okay. What would you like?"

"Let's see." One pale-pink tipped finger touching her chin, Gus pivoted on her heel and paced the perimeter of the shop, studying the various vases and table-top sculptures displayed on the shelves. Finally, she stopped in front of a vivid purple glass orchid which melted into tentacles at the tips of its petals. "I think I'd like this one."

It seemed very Gus, though Marco couldn't have said why. He nodded. "It's yours, then. Darryl? Wrap it up for her, would you?"

"Happy to." Darryl shot Gus a smile several shades warmer than any other woman would get from him, which was saying something. Gus smiled back, her eyes shining.

Marco watched the two of them with a growing suspicion as he rang up the Hidden Truths orchid, as he'd privately dubbed it. Evidently he'd been spending more time than he realized in the hot shop, if he hadn't even noticed these two hooking up.

What the hell. They could be good for each other. Or at least Gus would be good for Darryl. He wasn't entirely sure what Gus got out of it, but Darryl was a good man, smart and thoughtful even if he *did* have a roving eye. Gus knew what she wanted and she could handle him. She needed less worrying over than anyone Marco had ever known.

Gus walked over, set her purse on the counter and took out her credit card. She handed it to Marco. "How's the new light fixture coming along?"

"It's almost finished." He swiped her card and handed it back to her. "I was thinking I could maybe come out Friday to hang it. If that's okay with Darryl?"

"I guess so." Darryl leaned one hip against the counter. "You think you can wait 'til after four?"

Marco stifled a laugh. For some reason, their business usually fell off in the late afternoon on Fridays and Saturdays. Darryl intensely disliked being in charge of the shop when it was busy.

"Yeah, that's fine, as long as it still works for Gus and Rik." Marco raised his eyebrows at Gus. "So? What about it?"

"That's fine with me. I'll be here in town anyway. I have a meeting. But Rikky'll be home. He can help you hang it." She reached out to squeeze his wrist. "He'll be happy to see you."

To Marco's horror, he felt the goofiest grin ever spread over his face. "Yeah, well. It's mutual. It's been too long since I made the trip up the mountain."

The look on Gus's face said she knew exactly what Marco was thinking, but she kept it to herself. Good thing, too, since Marco didn't particularly want to listen to Darryl's inevitable teasing if he found out about Rik.

Of course, now that he'd figured out Darryl and Gus had hooked up, Marco had ammunition to fire back. Which he might need, if Darryl's expression was anything to go by.

Marco aimed what he hoped was a sufficiently quelling glare at his assistant. Darryl pressed his lips together and raised both hands palms-out in a gesture of surrender.

Gus tucked her credit card into her purse, picked up the bag with the glass orchid in it and hung it on her arm. She settled her purse over her shoulder. "Okay. Well, I need to get going. I have errands to run." Crossing to where Darryl stood, she took his hand. "I do believe Marco's figured us out, so…" She tilted her head up and sideways to plant a kiss on his lips. "Are we still on for tonight?"

"Yeah." Darryl darted a swift, guilty look at Marco, then favored Gus with his patented killer grin. He pressed her fingers with his. "I'll call you before I leave the shop."

"All right. See you then." With a bright smile, she let go of

Darryl's hand and turned to leave. She waved at Marco. "Bye, Marco. I'll tell Rikky you said hi."

"Great, thanks. See you later."

After she'd left, he rested his elbows on the counter and peered after her in thoughtful silence. "So," he said after a while. "You and Gus, huh?"

"Um. Yeah." Darryl eased himself down onto the other barstool they'd put behind the register. "Are you mad?"

Why Marco found that funny, he had no clue. Maybe because Darryl sounded so much like a high school kid who'd gotten caught driving his dad's car without permission. Whatever the reason, Marco laughed. "No, I'm not mad. What right would I have to be mad, anyway? You're both grown-ups. You can do what you want."

"Yeah." Darryl laced his fingers together in his lap and circled his thumbs around one another. He looked up at Marco with obvious curiosity. "So. You and Henrik?"

Marco's cheeks heated, though he couldn't think of a single reason why he should be embarrassed. "Looks that way."

Darryl nodded, his expression thoughtful. "Gus showed me pictures. He's a good-looking dude, and she says he's really smart. I guess he's worthy of you."

Touched, Marco clapped Darryl on the shoulder. "Thanks, man. He's…" *Beautiful. Special. Like no one else.* "He's unique. And you know me, run-of-the-mill just won't do."

He got a full-throated laugh in reply. "Nothing wrong with high standards, you know."

The shop door opened, bell jangling. A group of three middle-aged couples wandered in. Marco waved. "Hi, folks. Welcome to Furnace Glassworks. Let us know if you need any help."

One of the men pointed to a double-helix sculpture of iron and various colored glass. "I love this piece. Is it for sale?"

In fact, Marco hadn't planned to sell it, but hell, he had no particular emotional investment in it either. He smiled. "It can be, if you want."

The man grinned, eyes gleaming, and Marco resisted the urge to face-palm. Christ, he hated dealing with natural barterers.

Luckily, he employed one. He glanced at Darryl, who chuckled and hopped down from the stool. "Don't worry, Boss, I got this."

While Darryl sauntered over to the waiting customer, his most winning smile firmly in place, Marco slipped into the corner next to the office door, took his phone out of his jeans pocket and sent a text to Rik.

Coming up Fri eve 2 put in ur new lite. Saw G, sez she wont be home. I can stay if U want.

He waited. Minutes passed. Darryl finished his negotiations and was ringing up the sale—for a very nice price, too—when Marco's phone buzzed with a return text.

Yes. I'm ready.

Funny how three little words—not even the *big* three little words—could make a man's knees weak and his stomach turn somersaults.

Marco stuck his phone back in his pocket and sat before he could embarrass himself by falling over. God, but Friday was going to take forever getting here.

§ § §

Friday felt like it would never arrive. When the day dawned at last, Henrik didn't know whether to run through the house whooping in celebration or take a nap. The endless days of anticipation had him on edge and frazzled.

In the end, he rolled out of bed and headed for the gym, too restless to sleep and too unsettled in his gut to go for a run. Maybe some lifting would work off his excess energy and calm his mind. It could certainly use calming right about now.

Ever since Marco's text message on Tuesday, his brain had been stuck in the same endless loop, thinking about Friday—*today*—and what would happen then. Marco would come back up the mountain, back to the estate, with his dark eyes and his soft, wet mouth and his strong hands, and he'd take Henrik to bed and do all the things he'd described all those times on the phone. He'd let Henrik do things, too, let him touch and kiss and lick wherever he wanted. *Anything you want*, he'd promised in that growly, sexy voice. *Any way you want it.*

The memory sent a pleasant shudder down Henrik's spine. He leaned against the gym door and stared at nothing, seeing Marco's face instead.

"I'm going to have sex with Marco," he whispered, as if saying it out loud made it more real.

Sex. Not phone sex, but *real* sex.

Every time he thought about it, his heart tried to hammer its way out of his chest and he was afraid he might be sick. But he wanted it so badly he couldn't see past it. If Marco were to change his mind, Henrik had no idea what he'd do. Life beyond that possibility seemed utterly blank.

It scared him to feel that way. To have his entire being so completely focused on this one thing. To need it so much he couldn't imagine how he'd go on without it.

Irritated with himself, he shoved away from the door and stalked into the gym. He was being stupid. Of course he could live without sex. He'd done it this long, hadn't he?

Besides, Marco wouldn't change his mind. He'd be here this evening, not just to deliver the new light, but to show Henrik what sex was all about. He wanted it as much as Henrik did. It was clear as glass in his voice every time he spoke to Henrik on the phone. And when he'd been here in person the last time, when he'd looked at Henrik with those deep brown eyes full of heat and desire…

No. He wouldn't change his mind. Henrik knew it as surely as he knew where he'd wake up tomorrow.

Shaking his head as if he could knock Marco loose from his brain, he went to the music system, put his Deadmau5 collection on shuffle and turned his attention to his weights.

Henrik was in the kitchen making stuffed mushroom caps—his third recipe that afternoon—when Gus came in dressed for going out. She studied the trays of cookies, appetizers and spinach quiche covering the counters. "Wow. You've been busy."

"I've done all the exercise I can usefully do in one day and the house was already clean. Cooking was the only thing left to distract me." He took the sheet full of mushrooms, stuck it in the oven and set the timer. "Are you leaving already?"

Her eyebrows shot up. "You must've distracted yourself really well. It's four-thirty."

"What?" Leaning over the counter, he peered at the clock on the breakfast nook wall. "It is. Crap." He straightened up and met Gus's gaze. His hands shook with a sudden rush of adrenaline. "Wow. I didn't realize it was so late already." He picked up the half-empty glass of zinfandel he'd poured himself and took a healthy swallow.

All traces of teasing vanished from Gus's face. She strode forward, plucked the glass from Henrik's hand and set it on the counter, then put her arms around him and hugged him hard. "Marco's a great guy. You know he won't do anything you don't want him to. It'll be okay."

Holding her tight, Henrik smiled against Gus's hair. Of course she knew. She always knew.

"You're right." He kissed her cheek as she pulled away. "Be safe, okay? I'll see you tomorrow."

"Okay." Smiling, she squeezed his hand. "Bye, Rikky. Love you." She pointed a stern finger at his zinfandel. "And please stop at one glass, would you?"

Her tone was light, but he heard the very real worry behind it. If Marco wasn't going to be here in less than an hour, Henrik figured she'd cancel her meeting—and drop whatever hook-up she had planned for afterward—and stay to make sure he didn't do anything stupid. Never mind that it had only been that once, seven years ago, and it had turned out all right in the end. Although Gus would not hesitate to point out that it might not have, if she hadn't come home from London early and found him in time to call an ambulance.

His psychiatrist hadn't prescribed him Xanax again until she was satisfied he wouldn't swallow another two weeks worth and wash it down with a couple bottles of wine.

He gave Gus a wry smile. "Don't worry, I'm fine. Love you too." He gave her a light shove. "Go on. Have fun."

She studied him for a moment, nodded and walked away, her purse over her shoulder and car keys in hand. Watching her go, he wished with everything in him that he could leave, too. Just get in the car, drive to town and walk down the street like a normal person. Simply picturing it in his head made his breath catch and his pulse speed up, though. He knew he'd never be able to do it in reality, even if he ever learned how to drive.

He thought he'd come to terms with his limitations ages ago. This sudden longing to leave the estate, to experience the Outside and be like everyone else, bothered him. Partly because it disrupted his normally peaceful existence, but mostly because he had no idea why the helpless yearning and resentment he'd thought he'd overcome long ago chose *now* to unbury themselves.

He nearly jumped out of his skin when the oven timer beeped. God, had fifteen minutes passed already? Nervous and shaky all over again, he turned off the oven, grabbed a hot pad and took out the tray of mushrooms. They smelled wonderful. Hopefully Marco would like them.

Not to mention all the other things Henrik had spent the afternoon cooking.

He shook his head. If Marco didn't think he was completely nuts, he'd count himself lucky.

Oh well. Too late to worry about it now.

Leaving the mushrooms on the counter to cool, he took his wine and headed to his suite for a shower.

§ § §

The shower didn't relax him the way he'd hoped it would. He

thought about pouring another glass of wine, but he didn't really want any more. Besides, he had a feeling that wouldn't do any good either.

He was nervous. No denying it, and no getting around it.

The doorbell rang at twelve minutes after five. Henrik walked to the front door on weak, trembling legs and opened it before he had time to get himself any more worked up about it than he already was.

The sight of Marco on the other side, stunning in black jeans and a form-fitting dark gray shirt, ramped up Henrik's excitement to a near-painful level, yet calmed his anxiety at the same time. He smiled. "Hi, Marco."

"Hi." Marco's dark eyes dipped downward, surveying Henrik head to toe. He liked what he saw, if the way he smiled when he brushed past Henrik into the foyer was any indication. He set the large bag he carried on the floor, stepped closer to Henrik and touched his arm. "You look incredible."

Heat rose in Henrik's cheeks. He ran his palms over his newest jeans and the casual-but-nice royal blue button-down shirt. "Thanks." Feeling bold, he laid a hand on Marco's hip. "I missed you."

Marco let out a ragged breath. He slipped both arms around Henrik's waist and pulled him close. "I missed you too." He rubbed his cheek against Henrik's, stubble scraping his skin. "I really want to kiss you right now."

A hard jolt hit Henrik low in the gut. Unwilling to stop himself even if he could, he cradled Marco's face in both hands and kissed him the way they both wanted.

God, it felt *so* good. All of it. The soft, wet slide of Marco's tongue on his, the solid warmth of Marco's body pressed tight against him, Marco's low growl that sounded every bit as needy as Henrik felt. Even Marco's musky cologne and the rasp of his goatee on Henrik's skin felt unbearably exciting. He moaned and pressed closer, wanting everything all at once and not sure how to get it.

Marco's fingers dug hard into the muscles of Henrik's back. His mouth slid sideways, trailing kisses over Henrik's jaw and down his neck. "I think we need to take the edge off, babe."

His brain hazed with pleasure and desire, Henrik couldn't quite make sense of Marco's words. "Hm?" He wormed a hand down between them, up and under Marco's shirt. The smooth heat of Marco's bare skin against his palm tore a helpless *oh* from his throat.

"Shit." Marco tightened his arm around Henrik and walked him backward until his back hit the foyer wall. The look in Marco's eyes made Henrik feel hot all over. "I've been dying to do this for days. Brace yourself."

Before Henrik could process what was happening, Marco sank to his knees and pressed his open mouth to Henrik's crotch. Henrik's eyes rolled back in his skull. "Oh, God. Oh." He grasped at Marco's close-cropped hair.

"Shh. It's okay." Marco's voice was quiet, his breath warm and damp on Henrik's belly as he opened Henrik's jeans and worked them down over his hips along with his underwear. "I won't if you don't want me to. But I really, really want to."

Strong, sure fingers curled around Henrik's cock. He blinked, looked down and met Marco's gaze. He couldn't make a sound no matter how badly he wanted to, so he arched his hips toward Marco's mouth. Dark eyes shining, Marco slid his lips over the head of Henrik's cock and swallowed him down.

Henrik let out a wordless cry. The slick, wet heat of Marco's mouth scrambled his senses and turned his brain to sludge. He couldn't think, couldn't speak, couldn't do anything but clutch at Marco's head and try to stay upright while Marco made him feel better than he'd ever believed possible.

The familiar tight tingle of impending orgasm coiled between his legs before he was ready. He didn't want this to end. Not yet. But the feeling was too strong to fight. He came so hard his lungs seized up, leaving him voiceless, breathless and shaking against the foyer wall, his fingers digging into the skin of Marco's head while his cock pumped his release down Marco's throat.

Marco swallowed like it was easy, one arm clamped over Henrik's hips and the other hand rubbing soothing circles on his thigh. When Henrik's knees buckled, Marco pulled off, eased him to the floor and kissed him. It took him a moment to realize the odd bitter taste was the remains of his semen in Marco's mouth. The knowledge made his heart beat faster. He opened wider, delved his tongue deeper, chasing more of that strangely exhilarating flavor.

The kiss broke when Marco's lips curved into a smile. He stroked his thumb along the softening length of Henrik's shaft, making him shiver. "Good, huh?"

Henrik nodded. *Good* didn't seem an adequate description for what he'd just experienced, but his pleasure-hazed mind couldn't come up with a better one. He peered into Marco's eyes, hoping to convey how he felt with a look. Marco's cheeks were flushed, his lips red and swollen, his gaze heavy with unfulfilled need.

Oh, God.

Henrik's stomach rolled over. He'd daydreamed plenty of times about having Marco's cock in his mouth. Faced with the reality of it, however, he realized he had no idea what to do. He couldn't possibly measure up to Marco's skill. If Marco went soft in his mouth, he thought he'd die of humiliation.

You have to try. Just do it.

At least Marco wouldn't make fun of him. Right?

Heart racing with mingled fear and excitement, Henrik laid a shaking hand over Marco's crotch. Marco's eyelids fluttered to half-mast. He thrust against Henrik's palm with a low moan. Encouraged, Henrik fumbled the black jeans open. Marco lifted up to help get the jeans and underwear pulled down, and Henrik got his first real-life look at another man's privates.

It wasn't much bigger than his own, but it seemed much more intimidating. A little shorter, a little thicker. Foreskin still intact, unlike Henrik's. Cock and balls were both several shades darker than Marco's flat belly and groin. The skin over the shaft looked smooth, soft and delicate. Touchable.

Henrik ran his fingertips through the dark hair around the base of Marco's cock, over the tight balls, up the hard shaft to the exposed head. He ran his thumb over the glistening tip. It felt warm, silky and slightly damp. Even better, the touch made Marco shudder, groan and lift his hips. "God, Rik."

Henrik licked his lips, his throat suddenly dry as sand. He wrapped his hand around Marco's cock. It felt heavy, hot and alive in his palm, and he loved the contrast of the dusky skin with own pale fingers.

He leaned forward. Breathed deep. A sharp, wild scent hit him, and that did it. The need to root out the origin of that electrifying smell hooked him, drew him down and wouldn't let go until he'd caught the head of Marco's cock in his mouth and raked his tongue over the slit.

"Ah! Oh my God." Marco's body shifted. His fingers wove into Henrik's hair and tugged until he was forced to draw back. He gazed at Marco, wondering what he'd done wrong. Marco gave him a dazed smile and touched his cheek. "You don't have to. And… Well, I'm no virgin."

"Oh." Henrik looked away, cheeks burning. Of course someone as experienced as Marco wouldn't want a blow job from someone like him. He'd be clumsy and terrible.

"No. God, no, not that." Planting both hands on Henrik's face, Marco forced him to turn so they were eye to eye. He pinned Henrik with an intense stare. "I never wanted anything more in my whole fucking *life* than I want that gorgeous mouth of yours on my cock right now. Okay?"

It didn't even occur to Henrik not to believe him. "Okay. Then, why—?"

"Think about it, Rik. I've been with a *lot* of men in my life. I get tested regularly, and I'm negative for everything, but still." Marco caressed the corners of Henrik's mouth with his thumbs. His eyes followed the movement. "You should never take anybody's word for it when they say they don't have any diseases, you know?"

Henrik got it, finally, and laughed. Marco worrying over his health was *so* much better than Marco not wanting him to play because of his inexperience.

Tilting his head, he kissed Marco, because he couldn't *not.* "I want to make you come," he murmured against Marco's lips. He tightened the fingers still folded around Marco's erection, resulting in a soft curse from Marco. "If you won't come in my mouth, then it'll have to be something else." He gave Marco's cock a tug. Marco breathed a nearly soundless *oh fuck* into his mouth. He did it again, his whole body alive with a sense of power like he'd never felt before. "You can fuck me, if you want."

A hard shudder ran through Marco's body. The hand that had wandered into Henrik's hair tightened to the point of pain, but Henrik didn't care. He'd do *anything* for this feeling—to be the one bringing Marco to the brink. Making him lose control.

Marco shook his head, his eyes wide and frantic. "Not yet. Just…" Laying a hand over Henrik's on his cock, he thrust his hips upward.

Henrik got the message. Resting his head against Marco's so he could watch, he shifted his grip and stroked Marco's cock the way he'd do to himself when he was ready to come.

It didn't take long. Marco scrunched up his face and let out a sound almost like pain when he came. Henrik kept his eyes wide open, his gaze darting between Marco's face and the white fluid pulsing from his cock. He didn't want to miss a second.

He didn't let go until Marco collapsed against his side and shoved his hand away. "Mm. Too sensitive."

That, Henrik understood. He wiped his hand on his jeans—still down around his thighs, he was somewhat surprised to notice—and wound both arms around Marco's shoulders. "Was that okay?"

Marco laughed. He sounded breathless. "Oh, yeah, I'd say that was pretty okay. More than okay." Lifting his face, he favored Henrik with a goofy grin. "I hope you got more in you, though, because I had bigger plans for you than a quickie in the foyer." He stretched upward to nip at Henrik's jaw. "You're too fucking sexy for your own good."

A feeling too big for words took root and expanded in Henrik's chest. He beamed at Marco. "Oh, we are *definitely* not through. You're not getting out of here until you fuck me."

The expression that flared to life in Marco's eyes—heat, tenderness, affection, all shot through with a thread of fear—made Henrik's heart thud hard enough to hurt. Marco smiled. "Whatever you want, beautiful." He brushed Henrik's hair out of his face and kissed his nose. "In the meantime, how about we get cleaned up and hang your new light, huh?"

A whole new kind of excitement made Henrik sit up straighter. "Oh, yeah! I can't wait to see it. Oh, and I've been cooking all afternoon. So, we have food, if you're hungry."

Marco raised an eyebrow, but didn't ask questions. He grinned. "I knew something smelled good in here, other than you." He swooped in for a quick kiss before pulling away. "Okay, now that you mentioned food, I'm starving. Can we eat first, then hang the light?"

Right on cue, Henrik's stomach rumbled. He laughed along with Marco. "Yeah, let's eat. Come on."

They rose and hobbled into the kitchen with their pants around their thighs, snickering at how funny they must look. Instead of self-consciousness, Henrik reveled in a sense of camaraderie and shared experience. He'd never felt anything quite like it. Not even with Gus.

Sharing a warm washcloth and occasional kisses with Marco while they cleaned up, he said a silent prayer to whoever was listening that he'd never have to give up what he'd found today.

Chapter Seven

Marco popped the last of the stuffed mushrooms into his mouth with a happy hum. He closed his eyes while he swallowed, the better to savor the taste, then opened them and slumped back into his chair with a deep sigh. "Rik, you're an *amazing* cook. That was the best meal I've had in forever."

Henrik blushed a fetching shade of fuchsia, but his smile suggested he knew exactly how good he was in the kitchen. "Thanks. It was all the result of nervous cooking, though. If I'd been thinking at all, I'd've made a *real* meal instead of a bunch of snacks."

"Hey, quiche is real food, so there you go." Enchanted by Henrik's laugh, Marco leaned forward, took Henrik's hand and squeezed it. "You ready to hang the light?"

"Absolutely." Henrik rose, his hand clutching Marco's, his eyes bright and his cheeks still pink. "Come on. I'm anxious to see it."

Marco stood, keeping his fingers linked with Rik's. They went back to the dining room hand in hand. Before letting go to take the light fixture out of the bag, Marco pulled Rik close and kissed him. He didn't think about it. Didn't plan it. He just did it because it felt right. The way Rik looked at him afterward told him they were on the same page.

He did his best to tune out the warning voice in the back of his mind telling him it was way too soon to get this comfortable with anyone, never mind an agoraphobic virgin. Hell, chances were pretty damn good Rik was just using him as a way to get laid.

Yeah. Because he doesn't have the cash to get sex home delivered whenever he wants it.

Marco shook off the uncomfortable thought. Paying a professional to deflower them didn't appeal to most people. Even men liked a little romance in their lives, especially the first time.

Henrik's brow creased. "Marco? What's wrong?"

Shit. Smiling, he touched Rik's cheek. "Nothing. Just thinking about what happened when I got here." He raked his fingers through Rik's hair, just to watch it fall back over his face. "Nothing's hotter than a man who has to have it in the foyer."

There went that gorgeous blush again, making Marco's heart thump hard. Rik smiled, sweet, shy, and sexy. He wound his arms around Marco's neck. "I'd been thinking about all the things you told me on the phone. All the things you said you wanted to do with me." He mouthed the angle of Marco's jaw. Traced the shell of Marco's ear with his tongue. "I want all of that. I want you to do those things to me. I want to do those things to *you*."

Marco's vision blurred. "Oh Christ." He clung to Rik, for sheer physical support as much as the need to keep him close. "We have to get that light up *now*, or it has to wait until morning. Because I really, really want to take you to bed right now."

He felt Rik's breath run out in a rush on his neck. Rik pressed a gentle kiss to the spot just above his pulse point that always made him shiver, then drew back, blue eyes hazed with the same desire Marco felt. "Light first. I've been dying to see this thing, and I'm not waiting one minute longer."

Marco wasn't too sure he ought to mess with electricity while under the influence of Henrik, but he nodded anyway. "All right. Let's get this done, then you can show me your bedroom."

A wide, wicked grin spread over Rik's face. Pulling out of Marco's embrace, he made a beeline for the bag Marco had left next to the front door. He opened it, reached inside with both hands and lifted the fixture by its iron ring.

If he saw what else Marco had in the bag, he didn't say so. Marco was grateful for that. Now wasn't the time.

"Oh, wow." Holding it at arm's length, Rik studied the glass beads shot through with occasional streaks of pure sky blue. "This is beautiful, Marco. Just beautiful."

The admiration on Rik's face made Marco feel warm in ways that had nothing to do with sex. "Thanks. I loved working on it." He walked over and lifted a strand of beads, letting them run through his fingers. The fact that the blue wisps matched Rik's eyes was no accident. "I think this is one of my favorite pieces I've done."

"Really?"

"Yeah." Marco touched Rik's arm, admiring the feel of firm muscles beneath his shirt. "You got tools? I'll take down that old chandelier and you can help me hang the new one."

"Yeah. I set them out earlier." Rik nodded toward the archway to the formal living room.

Marco looked. A tool box sat on the floor beside the wall. He strode over, picked it up, set it on the table and opened it. Everything he needed was inside, neatly organized. He nodded his approval. "Nice. You stock a mean tool box."

Rik laughed. "You can thank Gus for that. She taught herself how to fix everything under the sun when she was a kid, and passed her knowledge on to me. She makes sure we have everything we need."

"I'm starting to think there's nothing she can't do." Marco took the things he knew he'd need and laid them on the table. "We'll have to cut off power to the light. Where's your circuit breaker?"

"In the basement. I'll get it." Rik trotted toward the door.

Marco frowned. "Maybe I should—"

"Marco. I can handle it." Rik stopped with one hand on the arch leading to the kitchen and grinned at Marco. "This house has a *lot* of circuits, as you might imagine. I know exactly which one controls this room. You'd have to hunt. And believe it or not, I know how the circuit breaker works. Trust me, okay?"

Something in Rik's eyes told Marco his answer held an importance beyond simple safety in hooking up the new light. Abandoning the tools, he went to Rik and cupped his face in both hands. "I do trust you. Completely." He kissed Rik's lips and let him go. "You take care of the electricity. I'll get everything set up here."

Rik touched Marco's hand then turned and jogged off, beaming. Marco watched until Henrik bounded through the door between the kitchen and the mud room. Once he was out of sight, Marco turned back to the tools and the new chandelier laid out on the table.

His mind went over the routine of taking down an old light fixture and hanging a new one without any problem. But he couldn't shake the unfamiliar warmth blossoming in his chest. Couldn't fight the feeling that he belonged here, somehow.

§ § §

"Okay, that's it." Climbing down from the stepladder Rik had helpfully provided, Marco put his hands on his hips and peered up at the new fixture with pride. "What d'you think?"

Rik stared, wide-eyed. "It's *gorgeous*. Wow." He turned to Marco with excitement practically shooting off him in visible sparks. "I have to go turn the electricity back on so we can see. Be right back." He swooped in to plant a hard, swift kiss on Marco's mouth, then set off for the basement at a dead run before Marco could move a muscle.

Chuckling, Marco walked over to the table—off center now, since he and Rik had moved it to hang the light—and leaned against it. He'd never met anyone as charming and absolutely guileless as Henrik. Which sort of scared him, when he thought about the two of them having sex.

A sharp thrill raised gooseflesh on Marco's arms. The things he and Rik had said to each other on the phone…God. You'd never know Rik was a virgin. But he *was*. He'd only ever seen those acts on porn sites online, only ever heard Marco tell him what it would feel like in real life. Marco's own life history had taught him that words and video could only prepare you so much. The reality of it—the true extent of the pleasure, and sometimes the discomfort—couldn't be explained. It could only be experienced.

Part of him didn't want to be the one to take Rik's innocence, because he wasn't sure he was worthy. But another, darker part of him *ached* to do it, to make Rik dream about it for the rest of his life.

The fact that Rik wanted him to be the one meant that his baser urges would be satisfied. No matter how hard he looked, he couldn't find any part of himself that honestly regretted it.

Henrik bounced back into the room carrying a bottle of champagne and two glasses, startling Marco out of his thoughts. "Okay, the electricity's back on." Rik held out one hand. "Hang on, I'm opening the champagne."

A close look at the label told Marco it was *real* champagne, from the right region of France. He raised his eyebrows. "Awesome."

Grinning, Henrik peeled off the foil, untwisted the wire and eased the cork out. He had an expert's touch. The cork came free with a soft hiss. He poured golden liquid into the two glasses, then recorked the bottle and took it back into the kitchen. When he returned, he picked up his glass and nodded at Marco to take his.

Once they both had champagne in hand, Rik stood beside the light switch with an air of palpable excitement. "Ready?"

Marco forced back the urge to laugh and nodded. "Ready."

"All right." Teeth digging into his lower lip, Henrik flipped the switch.

Even Marco was surprised by how pretty the new fixture looked, the light sparkling through the glass beads and forming glittering pinpoints on the walls. The overall impression was exactly what he'd envisioned—fragile, delicate, ethereal, like a tiny rainstorm reflecting sunlight through the room.

He laughed out loud. "Just what I wanted." Turning to Rik, he lifted his glass. "What about it, Rik?"

Henrik gazed at the light for another few seconds, enchantment written all over his face. Blinking, he swiveled to face Marco and smiled. "It's perfect. Just perfect." Raising his glass, he clinked it against Marco's. "Cheers."

Marco echoed Rik, and the chime of crystal against crystal faded as they drank. Rik licked his lips when he lowered his glass, and that was all Marco could stand. He leaned in and kissed Rik.

Rik's lips opened on a low sigh, his tongue coming out to slide against Marco's. The tartness of the champagne tasted wonderfully different when taken from Rik's mouth. Marco dug his free hand into Rik's silky hair and tilted his head to kiss him deeper, the better to seek out all of his flavors.

After long, perfect ages of nothing but the heat of Rik's mouth, his sweet little pleasure noises and the press of his body against Marco's, Rik broke the kiss and pushed Marco back by the shoulder. "Wait. Stop."

Confused, Marco stared at Rik's flushed face and red, swollen lips. "Huh?"

To his shock, Rik flashed a purely evil grin. "I'm not losing my virginity in the dining room." He clamped a hand around Marco's wrist. "We're going to my bedroom. Come on."

"Oh. Yeah. Hang on a sec." Easing his arm from Rik's grip, Marco went to retrieve the box of condoms from the bag the light had been in, then hurried back to Rik's side. He pretended not to notice the way Rik's eyes went wide at the sight of the box with its picture of a foil-wrapped prophylactic flanked by two grinning would-be lovers. "Should we get the champagne bottle?"

"Sure." Rik gave him a nervous smile. "I have a freezer, ice and an ice bucket in my suite, so it'll keep."

In the kitchen, Rik fetched the champagne from the fridge and carried it to his suite. Marco strode beside him, the hand holding the condom box slung over Rik's shoulder. The rubbers practically in his face seemed to make Rik a little uncomfortable, but at the same time he was clearly happy to have Marco's arm around him, so Marco was glad he'd done it.

Once they reached Rik's rooms, Marco didn't even have to pretend to be impressed with the surroundings while Rik put the champagne on ice and composed himself. "Wow. This is something else."

"It used to be a guest suite when my grandparents first built this place. I took these rooms after they retired and moved to Europe. Gus and I never really have overnight guests. Except for the corporate retreats, but that's only once a year, and we have rooms upstairs for that. And Gus's Lances, but they stay with her." Rik switched off the lights, other than a couple of low-wattage lamps beside his private bar. They gave off a warm golden glow. Rik paced over to stand in front of Marco, set their glasses on the coffee table and took his hands. "We both know why we're here, Marco. Please don't make me wait any longer."

Marco's heart stopped, thudded back to life and raced fast enough to make him breathless. He slipped his arms around Rik's waist. "Where's the bed?"

Rik swallowed, the sound louder than a gunshot in Marco's ears. One hand gripping the waistband of Marco's jeans, Rik led him through a pocket door on the other side of the living area into a large, airy space with three floor-to-ceiling windows taking up one wall and a huge bed situated where a person could wake up and look straight outside upon waking.

It made sense. Rik, who loved the outdoors but feared crowds of people, would need such a place for his private sanctuary.

Something pulled tight around Marco's chest. Drawing Rik close, he dipped his head to kiss Rik's neck. He nibbled along the big tendon and basked in the resulting shivers running through Rik's body. "Let me undress you."

It seemed a safe enough request, since Rik had been naked in front of Marco before. Still, Rik tensed and shuddered in Marco's arms. "Okay." His voice emerged in a shaky whisper.

Gentle. Everything slow and gentle.

Marco tossed the box of condoms onto the bed. Rik watched it arc, fall and bounce onto the mattress before snapping his attention back to Marco. He gazed into Marco's eyes as if Marco held his life in his hands.

Moving with as much care as if each slip of his finger indeed carried Rik's fate, Marco undid Rik's shirt, one button at a time, then slid it off his shoulders. It fell to the floor without a sound. Rik stared at Marco with wide eyes full of equal parts fear and heat. Marco let his gaze slide down Rik's bare chest and belly, admiring every inch on the way. When his eyes locked with Rik's again, most of the fear had bled away.

His throat tight for reasons he couldn't explain, even to himself, Marco tilted his head to capture Rik's mouth in a slow, deep kiss. He spread his hands across Rik's chest, rubbing his thumbs over Rik's nipples until they hardened. Rik moaned, both hands kneading Marco's ass through his jeans.

Without breaking the kiss, Marco ran his palms down Rik's sides, traced his fingers around the front of Rik's pants and undid the button on his jeans. He waited a few seconds, tugged down the zipper and eased the pants over Rik's hips. Rik let out a tiny, distressed sound, but used one hand to help shove his jeans and underwear down and kicked them off.

Breathing a silent thanks to whatever deity watched over gay men deflowering their virgin lovers, Marco gathered Rik close, kissing him and stroking his back until his body relaxed in Marco's embrace. Getting naked for a cock up your ass was completely different from going around naked just because you like the feel of bare skin, or even for getting your first blow job. Marco understood that, even if he'd never experienced it quite that way himself. Maybe it didn't make much logical sense, but nothing about sex counted as logical anyway. Marco intended to give Rik all the time he needed to feel comfortable with this. Provided he hadn't changed his mind.

When Marco felt Rik flip open the button on his jeans and yank down the zipper, he smiled against Rik's lips. "Want to go to the bed now?"

"Take these off first." Pulling back enough to look Marco in the eye, Rik grabbed a handful of Marco's jeans and underwear and tugged them down to mid-thigh. His gaze dipped downward, then back up, heavy with desire. "Take them off, Marco. Take them *off*."

The lump lurking in Marco's throat all night swelled a little larger. Unsure what it meant, he ignored it and wriggled out of his pants and underwear. Together, he and Rik pulled his shirt off and tossed it on the floor with the other discarded clothes, and they stood naked in each other's arms.

Rik stared into his eyes with a kind of horrified wonder, both hands gripping Marco's shoulders with bruising force. Rik didn't say anything, but the look on his face said it all. His heartbeat thudded against Marco's chest, and his cock dug hot and hard into Marco's.

God, Marco would give anything to melt away the last of Rik's fear and turn him into a bundle of raw sensation. Make him shake and whimper with pleasure, forget everything else but how good sex could make him feel.

Marco backed toward the bed, keeping his arms around Rik's waist. Rik clung to Marco's shoulders and followed. The visible throb of the pulse in his throat beckoned Marco to kiss it, so he did.

"Oooh." Rik arched his neck, one hand sliding upward to cup the back of Marco's head. "Marco."

All of Rik's need, his excitement and his lingering anxiety, came through clear as a mountain stream in that single whispered word. Marco kissed his way to Rik's mouth and nibbled his lower lip. Rik smiled, exactly the reaction Marco was after. Letting his arms fall away from Rik's waist, Marco sat on the edge of the bed, leaned in and dug his tongue into Rik's navel just hard enough to shock a sharp cry from him.

Grinning, Marco scooted backward onto the huge mattress and lay back on his elbows. "C'mon over here, babe."

Rik's throat worked. He shuffled forward and climbed onto the bed one limb at a time. Right knee. Left hand, left knee. Right hand last, beginning a leisurely crawl toward Marco. The whole time, he stared into Marco's eyes like he'd crack into a thousand pieces if he looked away.

Marco reached out and gathered Rik to his chest as soon as he got close enough. Rik tilted his head for a kiss, which Marco gave gladly. Rik's arm hooked around Marco's neck and stayed there, tense and trembling, though Rik's mouth was every bit as open and eager as ever.

After several minutes spent doing nothing but kissing, Marco eased Rik onto his back, silencing his soft sound of alarm-slash-desire with a deeper stroke of his tongue and his fingers through Rik's hair.

"We don't have to," Marco murmured against Rik's lips. He traced his fingertips down Rik's neck, over his chest rising and falling too fast with his rapid breathing, and planted his palm on the center of Rik's firm, flat belly. He peered into the blue eyes bright with lust and a hint of dread lurking underneath. "I won't ever try to make you do anything you don't want to."

Confusion creased Rik's brow for a moment before he smiled. "I know. I trust you." His smile faded into a look wavering somewhere between vulnerable and sexual. "I don't want to be a virgin anymore, Marco. And I…I want it to be you." He sucked his lower lip into his mouth. Let it go. Took Marco's hand and slid it downward. "Now. Tonight."

Even though he'd already held Rik's cock in his palm—had taken it in his mouth, brought him off and tasted his come—something about wrapping his fingers around Rik's rigid prick while lying naked in bed with him felt different. Maybe it was being able to see his face this close—the way his cheeks flushed and his eyelids fluttered, the way his head tilted to the left, his chin lifting and his kiss-stung lips parting.

Good God, he's so beautiful. Enchanted, Marco stroked him again, again and again, just to watch the play of raw feeling over his features. Rik hid nothing, held nothing back. Marco had never known anyone like that, *ever*, and he found it incredibly sexy.

Rik stopped Marco with a hand on his wrist before he could get a good rhythm going. "No. Not like that."

With any other lover, Marco might've teased. Now, he

simply moved his hand to Rik's chest, leaned over and kissed those plump, tempting lips. "How, beautiful? I'll do anything you want. Any way you want it." He knew what Rik had said earlier. But here in the bedroom, at the proverbial moment of truth, he didn't expect Rik to honor declarations made in the foyer. Especially since the extent of Rik's real-world sexual experience so far had happened this very evening, in the foyer.

Rik drew a deep, shaking breath. Blew it out, warm on Marco's mouth. "I…I meant what I said before."

Marco's heart lurched. He stroked Rik's cheek. The skin there felt hot against Marco's fingers. "Are you sure? Because—"

"I'm sure." Planting both hands on Marco's shoulders, Rik pushed him back enough to look into his eyes. Rik's own were a little too wide, but clear and glittering with determination. "It's all I think about. Having your cock in me. I want it."

The simmer in Marco's groin burst into a full-on blaze. Groaning, he slid his hand downward again to caress the inside of Rik's thigh, where the skin grew satin-soft and sensitive enough to make him gasp and spread his legs. "God, I want that too." Marco nuzzled behind Rik's ear. Sucked at the lobe until Rik let out a near-soundless *oh* and squirmed in Marco's grip. "I've been wanting to fuck you so much it distracts me when I'm working." He traced the shell of Rik's ear with his tongue. "I almost sculpted your ass in glass the other day."

That got him a surprised laugh. "You're kidding."

"Uh-uh." Nudging Rik's left leg a little further out to the side, Marco used his thumb to explore the crease between thigh and groin. Rik moaned and sprawled his leg out as far as it would go. Marco took the opportunity to wet his fingers in his mouth and slide them up and down the crack of Rik's ass. "I was thinking about this absolutely *perfect* butt, and I actually started making a sculpture of it instead of the rocks I was supposed to be making."

This time, Rik didn't answer. He dug his heels into the bed and moved his hips in an obvious attempt to get Marco's fingers closer to his hole. When he flailed his left arm over his head,

Marco wasn't sure what to think of it until Rik's hand dove under his pillow and came out clutching a bottle of lube. His eyes focused on Marco long enough to shove the lube in his direction.

Marco didn't need words to understand what Rik was trying to say.

Pushing up on one elbow, Marco grabbed the lube, flipped open the lid with his thumb and poured a healthy amount into his palm. He closed the bottle and set it aside. He peered into Rik's scared, trusting, wanting eyes while he slid his slick hand between Rik's legs. "Keep breathing, babe. And for fuck's sake, tell me if I hurt you. I'll stop. Okay?"

Rik smiled like the sun coming out. "You won't hurt me."

For the first time in his life, Marco wondered if he could live up to a person's expectations of him. He'd never been with a virgin before. He'd only ever been with guys as rough and hard-ridden as himself.

Even his first time hadn't been anything special—a drunk fuck up against a wall behind a gay bar in Houston. He'd gotten in with a fake ID when he was sixteen. The guy had gone soft inside him, cussed a blue streak, punched him in the face like it was his fault, passed out on the ground and puked about a gallon. In that order.

Of course, he'd learned a few things since then. He could be gentle, and he sure as shit knew how to fuck a man and make it good. Henrik trusted him. He just had to trust himself.

Holding Rik's gaze, Marco pushed one lubed finger into Rik's body. Rik hummed and pulled his leg up to his chest. "Mmm. Feels good."

"Yeah." Marco pressed his finger deep, twisting to hit Rik's gland. He grinned when Rik yelped and jerked, his fingers fisting in the expensive bedding. "You like that?"

"That's…wow." A full-body shudder shook Rik head to toe when Marco nailed the sweet spot again. "More."

Heart hammering, Marco pulled his finger out and slid two

inside Rik's loosening hole. Rik drew in a sharp breath, one hand digging into Marco's leg. "Oh. God."

Oh God was right. Marco wasn't sure how much more he could take. He'd never wanted a man this badly in his life. But he'd gladly suffer a few minutes longer rather than risk hurting Rik. Never mind the butt plug. A plug wasn't a live cock, and Rik had said it wasn't a big one. He'd evidently never really hit the sweet spot with it, in any case. So Marco worked his fingers in and out, in and out, stretching Rik with slow caution.

Rik arched his neck and let out a low, helpless noise when Marco rubbed his gland again. "Marco. Now."

Forcing back the haze of desire long enough to think practically, Marco twisted his fingers inside Rik, pressed them deep and spread them apart, watching Rik's face for any signs of discomfort. Nothing showed in Rik's pink cheeks and glittering eyes but pure pleasure, and Marco relaxed a little. Still…

"You're sure?" Talking wasn't easy, when Marco wanted nothing more than to sink his cock inside Rik's body every bit as much as Rik wanted it. But he couldn't do it until he felt certain Rik was ready. "I don't want to hurt you."

"No, I'm ready." Rik groped along Marco's thigh, found his prick and curled his hand around it, pulling a groan from Marco's throat. "Please."

Rik's voice held nothing but a need as sharp as Marco's own, and the last of his hesitancy melted away. Slipping his fingers out of Rik's ass, Marco pushed up on his elbow, reached for the condoms he'd dropped on the mattress and wrestled one free of the box. Unwrapping it and rolling it on took way more concentration than it should have, on account of Rik's warm, damp palm squeezing Marco's shaft with a particularly distracting lack of rhythm, getting in the way in spite of Rik's obvious intent to help.

With the condom finally on, Marco found the lube, poured a good handful and thoroughly slicked both his cock and Rik's hole. He pried Rik's fingers off his prick and kissed the knuckles.

"Roll over on your stomach."

Rik blinked at him. "Huh?"

"It'll be better that way." Leaning forward, Marco kissed Rik's lips. "Trust me."

Rik's mouth curved into a languid smile. He turned over without a word, got his knees under him and lifted his butt in the air. He peered sideways at Marco with his blue eyes glinting through a curtain of pale hair.

Something caught hard in Marco's chest. He brushed the hair from Rik's face, tracing his fingertips over the angle of Rik's jaw and down his neck. Rik's eyes fluttered closed, his lashes catching on a fine blond strand still trailing over his forehead.

Good God, but he made a pretty picture. Marco moved to kneel behind Rik before he could think too hard about the peculiar warmth expanding inside him.

He slid two slippery fingers inside Rik one more time, just to make sure. Rik rocked backward with a low moan. "Marco. Come on."

Normally, Marco didn't like keeping his lovers waiting long enough to make them sound impatient. In this case, though, impatience was a good thing. Grinning, he leaned over and kissed the curve of Rik's spine. "Okay, babe." Sitting up on his knees, he tugged his fingers free, took hold of his cock and positioned the head at the tempting opening that seemed about like the gates of heaven right now. "Relax. Keep breathing."

Predictably, Rik tensed when Marco first breached him. Marco held still, one hand on Rik's hip and the other rubbing circles over his lower back, and murmured soothing nonsense while he waited for Rik's body to adjust.

When he felt the tightness begin to ease from the ring of muscle squeezing his cock, Marco pushed in a bit more. Rik gasped. "Oh, God. Yeah."

Encouraged, Marco pulled out just enough to get a good thrust going. Rik keened and balled his fists in the covers. Marco clung to Rik's hips, fighting the urge to ditch his careful control and fuck Rik as hard as he thought he wanted.

The determination to make this good for Rik kept Marco's movements steady and gentle. He picked up the pace when Rik pushed up on his hands and shoved his ass backward to force Marco's cock in deeper. When he changed the angle to nail Rik's gland, Rik rewarded him with a sharp cry and his body tightening almost to the point of pain around Marco's prick.

"Fuck." Biting his lip, Marco leaned forward over Rik's back, rested his weight on his left hand and wrapped his right hand around Rik's cock. Rik let out a tortured moan, and Marco made himself think through his to-do list back at the shop to keep from coming on the spot. "Okay?"

Rik nodded. "Feels good."

Marco peered at Rik's profile. His panting breaths dislodged a strand of shining blond from his bottom lip. The way it swung in front of his chin made him seem young and vulnerable.

Once again, the desire to give Rik a perfect first experience snagged Marco by the heart and shook him. Rik had waited such a long time, and he'd given the gift of his virginity to Marco. Marco intended to make sure Rik got nothing but the purest pleasure in return.

Skimming his hand up Rik's shaft, Marco ran the pad of his thumb over the head. Rik shuddered beneath him. Marco did it again, thrusting into Rik at just the right angle while his hand slid down Rik's cock and back up again, swiping at the sensitive head on the upstroke.

The muscles in Rik's back bunched as he dug his hands into the mattress like he might fall off the earth if he didn't hang on. "Faster. Go faster."

Parts of Marco wanted to shout *hallelujah*. The rapidly shrinking sensible parts of his brain held control of his tongue for the moment, however, and he did what Rik asked with nothing more than a heartfelt groan.

He felt the exact moment Rik started his final approach to

the magic moment. His body tightened around Marco's prick, his arms tensing until his shoulder blades stood out like wings trying to break through his skin. His cock, already hard, stiffened even more and swelled in Marco's hand. "God. I—Mar—"

His voice trailed into a sound Marco would've mistaken for pain if he didn't know better. Marco's pulse went from a trot to a full gallop, pounding with suffocating force at the base of his throat. Bracing himself with his feet and the hand planted on the mattress, he stopped holding back and slammed into Rik with everything he had, over and over until that unmistakable feeling grabbed him by the balls and slung him into the stars.

Rik came seconds later with a near-silent *oooh*, his body shaking beneath Marco's chest. Still caught up in his own orgasm, Marco rested his forehead on Rik's damp back and milked Rik's cock, whispering things he figured he ought not think too hard about while the warm, slick fluid flowed over his fingers.

Finally, after long, sweet minutes that Marco never wanted to end, Rik pushed Marco's hand away. "Mm. Too much."

Marco chuckled. "Gotcha." Forcing his double-weight post-orgasm body upright, he pulled out of Rik's body as slowly and carefully as he could, took off the condom and gave it a twirl. "You got a trash can I can hit without getting up?"

Laughing, Rik wriggled onto his side and grinned up at Marco. "Just toss it on the floor. I'll pick it up later."

"The floor?" Scandalized, Marco took a good look at the rich, gleaming hardwood on either side of Rik's bed. "You can't be serious."

Rik rolled his eyes. "That floor's got a really tough urethane finish. *Nothing* can hurt it. Trust me. Gus and I tried hard enough when we were kids, sneaking in here when this was a guest suite."

Marco shot Rik a narrow-eyed look. Rik raised his eyebrows. Marco sighed. "Okay."

He tossed the used condom over the side of the bed. It hit the well-finished hardwood floor with a wet *splat*.

Marco cringed. Rik grinned. "Relax, Marco." He shifted onto his back, took Marco's hand and tugged. "C'mere."

If Marco had a tough time resisting Rik before, he didn't stand a chance against Rik's after-sex look—all flushed, sweaty skin, mussed hair and sated, shining blue eyes. Marco went into Rik's embrace, into his pleasure-drugged kiss and a caress less innocent than before.

When he broke the kiss a glorious age later, Rik molded himself to Marco's side with a deep sigh, his face buried in the curve of Marco's neck. "That was amazing, Marco. Just...just wonderful. Perfect."

"For me, too." Marco wrapped both arms around Rik and held him tight, his cheek pressed to Rik's hair. "I didn't hurt you any?"

"Not at all." Slinging a leg over Marco's thighs, Rik branded Marco's throat with a lingering kiss. "Stay with me tonight."

It wasn't phrased as a question, but Marco heard the request in Rik's voice anyway—the uncertainty, now that they'd done the deed. The fear that Marco would leave, go back down the mountain and never return.

Marco didn't know how to feel about the fact that his unhesitating answer was "Yes."

Chapter Eight

Henrik had had plans for the rest of the night. He'd thought they'd cuddle up in bed together and watch a movie while they finished the champagne. Or they could take the bottle outside, relax in the hot tub and admire the stars. Later, they'd make love again, slow and sweet. Maybe he'd lie on his back this time, so he could wrap his legs around Marco's waist and look into his eyes when he came.

Instead, he fell asleep in Marco's arms and didn't wake until after dawn the next morning.

It was hard to regret it, though, when he drifted out of sleep to the exciting, unfamiliar feel of Marco's body curled around his back, Marco's arm snug around his waist and Marco's soft breathing on his neck. Smiling to himself, Henrik laid his hand over Marco's where it rested on his belly and wove their fingers together. Marco grumbled something unintelligible, snuggled closer and lay still. Lying spooned together in the morning light flooding through the eastern window, with Marco's body still limp and heavy in sleep, the press of his half-hard cock against Henrik's butt felt comforting rather than sexual.

Unlike last night.

Henrik closed his eyes, remembering. He'd known going in that he wouldn't be truly prepared for it. But he'd braced himself for discomfort. Pain, even. He'd mentally steeled himself for pushing through a certain amount of unpleasantness to get to the good stuff.

What he'd never foreseen was the discomfort being so brief and minimal, and the pleasure so overwhelming.

Henrik wasn't stupid, nor was he as naive as he knew he seemed. He was well aware that he owed his magnificent first sexual experience to the man currently drooling on his neck. Marco's skill, Marco's gentleness, and most of all the fact that Marco cared enough to make his first time wonderful.

He doesn't just want me. He cares about me.

That knowledge started Henrik's heart hammering more than any of the things they'd done last night, or any of things they'd whispered about over the phone. It frightened him, because he wasn't sure he measured up. Could he really be someone's lover? Not just in the physical sense, but in the sense of being their one-and-only. Now that he thought of it, did men even do that? Did they stay with one person? God only knew Gus didn't, but he'd already figured out that she was an unusual woman in countless ways. Now, lying naked in bed with a man on the morning after for the first time, Henrik realized he knew nothing about relationships in general or relationships between men in particular. Watching online gay porn was spectacularly unhelpful in that regard. He'd never seriously considered the idea of being with someone himself, and therefore hadn't even tried to learn anything beyond how to have sex.

He hoped his ignorance didn't end up souring the first truly good thing to come into his life since his agoraphobia diagnosis. For that matter, he hoped he wasn't setting himself up for heartbreak by even hoping for more than a night together. What if Marco never wanted to see him again, now that they'd had sex?

God, this was all way too confusing. He let out a deep sigh.

Behind him, Marco stirred and yawned. His arm tightened around Henrik's waist. "Good morning, beautiful." He planted a kiss on Henrik's neck. "How're you feeling?"

"Absolutely wonderful." Henrik turned his head to claim a proper kiss, mutual morning breath be damned. He grinned at Marco's half-asleep expression, doing his best not to let all his doubts and fears show on his face. "I've never woken up in bed with a naked man before. I like it."

Marco laughed. "Good, because this is happening again if I have any say in it." A furrow dug between his brows. "It doesn't have to, if you don't want. But I have to be honest here. Last night was fantastic for me, and I really want it to happen again. Preferably a *lot*."

Some of the anxiety in the back of Henrik's mind evaporated. Squirming onto his other side to face Marco, he wound his arms around Marco's neck. "This is definitely happening again. As soon and as often as you can come back up the mountain."

The wide, sexy smile that made Henrik's heart thud painfully hard broke out over Marco's face. Sliding one hand into Henrik's hair and the other downward to cup his ass, Marco tilted his head for a long, slow, lazy kiss.

Henrik tumbled into it, his head spinning with a dizzying mix of relief, apprehension and growing desire. He had no idea what lay ahead for the two of them, whether he'd eventually screw it up or they'd settle into something comfortably long-term. Maybe even grow old together. Whatever happened in the future, though, he intended to savor every precious second of the present while it lasted.

§ § §

Henrik was in the middle of a workout in the gym when his phone started playing Massive Attack's "Angel".

Marco. Grinning, Henrik set the weights back in their rack, reached for his phone and brought up the text message waiting for him. *hey babe. gonna B late 2nite. shops busy & i need 2 finish up some projects b4 i head ur way. hope thats ok.*

Disappointment settled like lead in the pit of Henrik's stomach. He hardly had room to complain, though. Not when Marco had gone out of his way to make the trip up the mountain no less than four times in the last ten days. Each time, he'd spent the evening talking and laughing and making love with Henrik, then stayed the night in his bed before heading back to town for another full day of work. Not once had he complained about the long drive or the fact that he always had to be the one to make the effort while Henrik sat at home and waited for him.

All things considered, Henrik thought himself lucky Marco hadn't canceled tonight.

No problem, Henrik messaged back. *Just glad you can come at all. See you when you get here.*

k. thx babe. ill bring takeout ;)

Henrik sent back a text saying he would cook. No return message arrived immediately, so he set the phone on the windowsill and went back to his workout.

When Marco still hadn't answered after almost fifteen minutes, Henrik knew they'd be having takeout tonight. Not because Marco hadn't seen the text—Henrik knew he had, he always did—but because he'd already decided to provide dinner. Probably to make up for being late, though he didn't need to as far as Henrik was concerned.

Shaking his head, Henrik turned off the stereo and headed for the shower.

Afterward, he took a bottle of water from the gym's small refrigerator and wandered through the door leading from the gym to one of the trailheads. The forest grew close here, but the afternoon sun beat down like a physical weight on the fifty feet or so of grass between the house and the trees. Sweat broke out on Henrik's brow.

He stepped out into the grass, which felt cool against his bare feet. A walk in the forest was tempting. A chilly early spring had given way to warmer than usual temperatures here at the tail end of May though, and the heat under the trees would be oppressive, especially if he had to put on clothes.

A swim. That sounded perfect. Taking a deep swallow from his water bottle, Henrik turned and strode off in the direction of the courtyard.

Finding Gus there didn't surprise him much. This was the only outdoor pool on the property—his grandparents hadn't liked swimming and had only kept pools for guests—so sharing it was understood. After all, it wasn't *actually* his, even if he and Gus both sort of thought of it that way. While he might've expected Gus to be here, however, he'd never expected to see a strange man with her.

He wasn't sure how to feel about it. This was Gus's house—

and Gus's pool—as much as it was his. Still, she'd always kept her Lances to her bedroom and the kitchen, and he couldn't help feeling blindsided.

Neither of them had noticed him hovering behind the landscaping. Squaring his shoulders, Henrik marched up to edge of the pool and planted his feet as close as he could to where Gus and her latest conquest floated on opposite sides of a blue foam raft, arms intertwined, legs drifting in the deep end of the water and gazes focused on one another. "Hi, Gus. Hi, Lance."

They both looked up. The man gaped for a second, then his handsome face broke into a wide smile. "You're Henrik! Marco talks about you all the time." He pulled an arm free, kicked closer to the edge and held his hand toward Henrik in roughly the same space of time it took Henrik to figure out who this was. "Darryl Fields. I work with Marco. Great to meet you, finally."

Not knowing what else to do, Henrik bent down, took Darryl's hand and shook. "Nice to meet you too, um, Darryl." He let go of the other man's hand and stood up straight, feeling at a loss for words. God, this was strange. Gus had never brought anyone but a Lance here before. "So…"

"Why'd you call me Lance?" Darryl gave Henrik a quick up-and-down glance. "Gus said if you were around you'd be running around in your birthday suit. That's cool. Everybody's gotta do their own thing, you know? I'm glad she warned me though." He grinned. "Hell, if I looked that good, I'd go around bare-assed too."

Gus laughed, her whole face glowing like a spotlight. "You *do* look that good, silly."

Darryl put on an obviously fake thoughtful expression. "Yeah, I guess I'm not half bad." He flexed his arm. Muscles bulged beneath the dark skin, sending water droplets sliding off into the pool. "Not as buff as your cousin, but not too shabby, I'd say."

Henrik gave the man in the pool—Darryl, not Lance; wow, that was one for the record books—a once-over. The parts of him visible above the water, anyway. He really was a good looking man. Handsome in a clean-cut, athletic way. And he hadn't been the least bit startled or put off by Henrik's nudity, which was unusual.

Most of all, though, he clearly considered Gus a goddess, judging by the way he looked at her. It won him a lot of points in Henrik's book. Since she seemed to think just as highly of Darryl—she'd brought him home, after all—Henrik decided to forget his lingering sense of resentment that she hadn't told him she was bringing company to the pool. After all she'd done for him over the years, marring her obvious happiness over such a small thing would be selfish and wrong.

She must have seen something in his face, though. He dove into the pool and surfaced on the far side, and she was right behind him, pulling up to the edge and hanging onto the concrete beside him. Henrik turned. Darryl had climbed up the ladder and was heading toward one of the lounge chairs.

Gus rested a hand on Henrik's arm before he could say anything. "I sent you a text to let you know Darryl was here and we were coming out to the pool. Didn't you get it?"

A text. Everything made sense now.

Smiling, he kissed the worried crease between her eyes. "I must've just missed it. I left my phone in the gym, like an idiot."

Relief smoothed the concern from her face, though she didn't release him from her keen stare. "You're handling this very well. Are you upset?"

Henrik gave the matter serious thought, and realized he wasn't. Not really. "No, I'm fine."

Her eyes narrowed. "You're sure?"

"I'm positive." He laughed at her suspicious expression. "I know I'm not usually this easy to live with, but Marco's been very good for me."

"I can see that." The corners of Gus's mouth tipped upward. "I'm glad. It's about time someone made you this happy."

"I could say the same." Henrik shot a glance at Darryl, who'd stretched out on a lounge chair with his hands tucked behind his head. "He'd better be good to you."

She smiled, radiating happiness like a supernova. "He's wonderful."

Gus didn't talk much about her love life, but the few conversations she'd had with Henrik had taught him plenty about the challenges she'd faced when it came to romance. Apparently far too many straight men took it as a personal affront if a woman as beautiful as Gus dared to possess intelligence, an impressive variety of skills and ambition beyond catching a man.

Nothing turned Gus off faster than possessiveness. If Darryl had ever shown any tendency to control her, he wouldn't be here right now.

Henrik grinned. "Good." Planting his feet on the pool's edge, he pushed off and backstroked to the other side. Gus paced him, and they reached the ladder at the same time. He wiped the water from his eyes. "Did he stay last night, or is he staying tonight?"

"Both. He's on vacation this week. He's heading home to see his parents tomorrow, but for right now he's all mine." A shadow fell over them. Gus looked up and laughed as Darryl jumped over their heads and splashed into the pool. "I thought you wanted to lie in the sun," she said when he surfaced.

"I did. It's too hot." His face full of mischief, Darryl swam closer. "Speaking of hot…" Growling, he bit Gus's neck.

She let out a surprised yip, turned and shoved Darryl underwater. He came up spluttering and laughing and ducked her in return. Henrik hung onto the ladder and stared in shock while his cousin engaged in a water battle and giggled like she hadn't done since they were children.

He'd never seen her this carefree and unreservedly joyful. It looked good on her.

She'd never blamed Henrik for the restrictions on her. As she'd said more than once, she'd *chosen* this life. She liked the privacy of the estate, as well as the inherent authority of running the company from home the way their grandfather had. Her choices weren't all about Henrik. Still, he knew he'd held her back. He just hadn't realized how much until now.

Feeling morose even though he knew he shouldn't, Henrik kicked off from the ladder and swam toward the shallow end of the pool. Maybe a few laps would settle his thoughts into something approaching good sense. The last thing he wanted was for Marco to arrive and find him wallowing in guilt and depression.

About the time he reached the curve of the stone steps leading into the three-foot-deep end of the pool, a thought struck him. If Darryl was here, that left Marco to handle the shop alone. Which was why he would be late tonight, and would no doubt have to leave early in the morning.

Henrik glanced at Darryl and Gus. They'd stopped trying to drown each other and were floating on the raft again, talking quietly and smiling at each other.

Pushing off the steps with both feet, Henrik swam as hard as he could. Try as he might, though, he couldn't escape the unfamiliar jealousy churning in his gut.

Chapter Nine

"Fuck. Yeah, babe. Oh." Marco clenched his fist in Rik's hair and hung on for dear life while he shot down Rik's throat.

When the orgasm loosened its grip on him—and Rik loosened his grip on Marco's cock—Marco's knees decided they were done holding him up. He slid down the wall to land in a heap on the floor of Rik's bedroom.

Rik grinned at him, smug as a man could be with red cheeks, tangled hair and semen running down his chin. "Pretty good, huh?"

Marco laughed, sounding exactly as breathless and well-sucked as he felt. Like Rik didn't know how amazing he'd gotten at sucking cock over the last month. "Jackass. C'mere."

Snickering, Rik tackled Marco onto his back and kissed him, mouth wide open and not one bit shy. The taste of his own come hit Marco's tongue, making him moan. He had no clue why he found that sexy, but damned if he didn't.

Only when he got it from Rik, though. He'd tried it ages ago after jerking off, when he was way younger and still willing to try anything and everything. Hadn't liked it much then, and hadn't liked it any better when he'd tried it again after learning how much better it tasted coming from Rik's mouth. For some reason it didn't taste the same unless he took it straight from Rik's soft, slick tongue.

Rik let out an impatient noise. His prick dug into the bend of Marco's hip. Breaking the kiss, Marco buried his face in Rik's neck to hide his smile. Rick couldn't have begged for a blow job any harder if he'd done it out loud.

Not that Marco minded. In fact, swallowing Rik's cock had quickly become one of his favorite things. Marco clamped his arms around Rik's waist and rolled him over.

One of these days, Rik would probably figure out how to

keep himself from coming so fast. But it had barely been a month since that first night in the foyer, and he didn't last any longer this time than he had any of the other times Marco had sucked him off.

Marco didn't care. He'd have gladly spent hours working Rik with lips and tongue, just to listen to his sweet moans and smell the sweat on his skin. The taste of Rik's release was icing on the cake, no matter how quickly it happened.

When Rik sighed and collapsed into a boneless sprawl, Marco reluctantly removed his head from Rik's crotch and crawled up for a kiss. Henrik opened to him just as eagerly as before, his mouth moving with his usual lazy post-sex languor.

A wonderful warmth expanded in Marco's chest. He loved these moments, with Rik warm and pliant in his arms, kissing him like there was no past, no future, nothing but the two of them here and now. He wished it would never end.

Nothing lasted forever, though. Least of all the good things. Rik pulled away after a few minutes and pressed his cheek to Marco's, both arms tight around Marco's neck.

Now that the orgasm-high had faded, Marco felt Rik's distraction even without seeing his face. Rik had been distracted a lot lately. Lost in his own thoughts any time the two of them weren't talking or fucking.

Something was bothering him. Marco didn't know what, but something had been on Rik's mind for a while now and he wasn't sharing it with Marco. He'd asked Rik once if anything was wrong. Rik had said no, which should've reassured Marco but instead only worried him more. No matter what Rik said, his face reflected his every emotion, and those expressive features told a different story from his words. As far as Marco knew, Rik had only ever deliberately lied to him that once. Marco had no idea *why*, though, and it prodded at the back of his mind until he'd become nearly as distracted as Rik.

He didn't know whether to blame it on fate or irony when Rik stirred and murmured in his ear, "Marco? Is something wrong?"

Marco laughed, though it wasn't funny. "Actually, I kind of wanted to talk to you about something," he said before he could lose his nerve.

"Oh. Okay." Rik's body tensed beneath his, fingers digging into his neck. "What is it?"

Marco pressed a gentle kiss to Rik's lips—because kisses said so much that words couldn't—then rolled off of Rik, lying propped on one elbow so he could see Rik's face. "Something's been bothering you lately, Rik. Last week when I asked you what was wrong, you said nothing was. But I know that wasn't true."

Rik's cheeks went bright pink. He looked away, eyes wide. "No, I—"

"Hey." Marco traced the line of Rik's jaw with his fingertips. "It's okay. I'm not mad at you or anything." *Just irritated.* He wasn't going to say that, though. Not with Rik looking like he might jump up and run any second. "I just want to help, if I can." He dragged his thumb over Rik's bottom lip. Rik's breath hitched, and Marco's not-quite-anger vanished like mist in the sunlight. He kissed Rik again, because he couldn't help himself. "Whatever it is, you can tell me."

Rik met his gaze again, blue eyes troubled. Marco watched him, stroked his hair and waited. Rik's forehead furrowed for a moment, then smoothed. He flashed a smile that looked painfully fake. "I'm fine. Honest."

Disappointment and renewed exasperation drove Marco to his feet, in spite of the way Rik's face fell when Marco pushed away from him. Rik's openness and honesty were the things that had attracted Marco to him from the first. Having Rik lie to him hurt way more than any of the other times he'd been lied to in the past. And he'd been lied to plenty.

Rik stood, went to Marco and took his hand. The gesture felt hesitant, something Rik had never been with Marco. "Okay, *now* you're mad at me."

What could he say? Marco could hardly bitch about Rik lying to him, then turn around and do the same thing to Rik.

Sighing, Marco squeezed Rik's hand. "A little, yeah."

"Oh." Rik gnawed his bottom lip. "Why?"

"It's kind of hard to explain." Boy, was *that* ever the understatement of the damn year. Marco wasn't sure his attitude made sense even to him, really. But he owed Rik at least an attempt at an explanation. He rubbed his free hand over his head. "Okay, this is probably gonna sound stupid. But you...you're like a diary someone left open on a table. You can't hide anything even when you try, and you don't ever try. And—" He stopped. Scrubbed his palm over his head again. The soft hairs tickled his palm. Damn, he really needed a haircut. He fought back an entirely inappropriate laugh, because fuck if this wasn't harder to say than he'd expected. "I *like* that about you, all right? I like it that you're so easy to read. I like that you don't hide things. It's always been my favorite thing about you. But you're hiding something now, and I hate that."

Marco wasn't sure what he'd expected to happen, but it wasn't Rik ripping his hand from Marco's, stalking across the room and pinning Marco with a venomous glare. "And what makes you think I have to tell you everything?"

Stunned, Marco shook his head. "That's not what I meant."

"Well, that's what it sounded like to me."

Rik sounded so unlike himself that the automatic argument died on Marco's tongue. He studied Rik, looking for what he wasn't saying. And there it was—in Rik's hunched posture, in the way his crossed his arms, in the unfamiliar belligerence in his expression.

Whatever was eating Rik, he was afraid to tell Marco about it. Why, Marco had no idea, but he knew fear when he saw it, and he was staring it in the face right now.

God, it made him tired. He went to the bed, flopped onto his back and stared up at the ceiling. "Look, you don't have to tell me anything if you don't want. But I'd rather you said outright that you don't want to tell me something, than to lie and say nothing's wrong when there obviously is."

Across the room, Rik stood silent for a while. Marco lay quiet and waited. After a several endless seconds, Rik shuffled to the bed, lay down beside Marco and took his hand. "Something's been bothering me. You're right. But I'd really rather not talk about it."

Marco laughed. "Well, I asked for that."

Rik's fingers tightened around Marco's. "I'm sorry."

He sounded honestly sorry, which made Marco ashamed of himself for making such a big deal out of the whole thing. He turned his head so he could see Rik's profile. "Don't be. It's your business whether you want to talk about stuff or not. I shouldn't've pushed."

Rik's lips curved into a solemn version of his usual smile. "It's okay."

They lay side by side in uncomfortable silence for a while, their hands still linked. Eventually, Rik let go, rolled over and kissed Marco. "It's getting late. I'll go start dinner." He pushed to his feet and headed for the door.

"I'll help." Marco stood, snatched his shorts from the floor, pulled them on and followed Rik.

To Marco's relief, the quiet between them on the way to the kitchen lacked the tension from before. But he still hadn't learned what had been stealing Rik's attention lately, and he didn't know what to do about that.

§ § §

Cant make it 2nite. Work piling up. Sorry babe. Ill make it up 2 u.

Henrik stared at the text message on his phone, his heart sinking. Marco had never canceled on him before.

Tucking his legs beneath him on the poolside lounge chair, Henrik thought for a minute, then messaged back, *It's ok. Let me know when you can come again. I'm not going anywhere ;)*

He didn't get an answer. Not that he expected one. References to his agoraphobia made Marco uncomfortable, so he'd learned not to make them. Joking about it in a text pretty much guaranteed that Marco wouldn't call again until tomorrow, or maybe even Friday.

Of course, Rik knew his ill-advised text joke wasn't the only thing keeping Marco at a distance lately. Something had been bothering him for quite a while now, though it had been more pronounced since their fight—if you could call it that—last Sunday. He'd been distracted when they were together, frowning whenever he believed Henrik wasn't watching. Worse, he hadn't been staying the night as often as he used to.

Actually, he'd only gone home instead of staying a couple of times, but Henrik couldn't help taking it as a kind of rejection, even though logically he knew Marco didn't mean it that way. The man ran a business, after all, and had his own place in town. He couldn't be expected to stay with Henrik all the time, or even half the time. But Henrik had never been in a relationship before. He had no idea what to expect, what was reasonable and what wasn't. Navigating the ins and outs of being with someone felt like stumbling his way through a maze blindfolded.

He thought he knew the cause of Marco's uncharacteristically pensive mood. He didn't ask, though, because he still didn't want to answer the questions he knew Marco would ask in return.

The irony of the situation did not escape him.

His phone rang, making him jump. Lifting his sunglasses, he peered at the display, and sighed. He thumbed on the phone. "I thought you were home already. Where are you?"

Gus made an impatient noise. "My tire pressure light came on just before I got to town. Apparently I picked up a roofing nail somewhere along the road. My car's in the shop getting a new tire. I'm at Furnace Glassworks with Darryl right now. I'm not sure what time I'll be home, but I *will* be home some time tonight, since I have that video board meeting in the morning."

"Okay." Henrik lay back in the lounge chair and studied his bare body with a critical eye. No redness yet, but he should probably go inside soon. Sunburn had a way of sneaking up on him, no matter how hard he tried to prevent it. "Tell Marco hi for me, as long as you're there."

"Oh, well, I just missed seeing him, but if he's back before I leave I'll be happy to tell him."

Henrik's stomach performed a slow, unpleasant roll. "He's not there?"

"No. Darryl said he went out to dinner with some friends." Gus's voice dropped into a low, sympathetic murmur. "I didn't say anything, but didn't you tell me this morning that Marco was coming up the mountain tonight?"

"He was supposed to, yes. He texted me a few minutes ago and said he couldn't make it because he had too much work to do."

Surprised silence met his announcement. His throat burned with the shame of being blown off by his first and only lover, but at least Gus would stand firmly on his side. He'd always been able to tell her anything, and he was profoundly grateful for that.

"Right now I really kind of want to kick his ass." This time, Gus's voice emerged clipped, measured, and deceptively calm. Henrik had heard her verbally eviscerate more than one incompetent corporate lackey in precisely that tone. "I can hang around for a while, if you want."

Henrik smiled, in spite of the ache in his chest. God, he loved her. No matter what happened with Marco, he counted himself a lucky man to have her on his side. "No, don't do that. And don't say anything to Darryl either, okay? I appreciate your willingness to beat people up for me, but it makes me feel just a little bit too much like a gangster for comfort if I send my cousin out to break a man's kneecaps just because he wasn't entirely honest about why he canceled a date."

Gus laughed, though the sound was laced with sadness. "I never said I'd break any kneecaps. But I see your point." She let out a soft sigh. "Anyway, maybe we're jumping to conclusions. Darryl said Marco was in the office all morning working on financial stuff for the shop, then he'd been working in the hot shop all afternoon. It's entirely possible that he's honestly just going to dinner with friends, then going back to work. Or even going home to rest, since I know he doesn't get any rest when he's with you."

Henrik couldn't deny it, though he wasn't about to feel bad about it either. He grinned, remembering all the not-resting he and Marco had done together over the past few weeks. "This is true."

"Smugness doesn't suit you, cousin." Gus sounded amused. "Seriously, though, don't you think we ought to give him the benefit of the doubt?"

Henrik resisted the urge to stare at his phone as if it were actually Gus. She was a reasonable person, but she tended toward protectiveness when it came to him. "I thought you wanted to kick his ass."

"I do. Still, I'm a very good judge of character and Marco simply doesn't strike me as a liar."

"Then why didn't he tell me he was out with his friends?" He sounded petulant, and hated it, but he couldn't seem to help it.

"Rikky. Listen to yourself. Don't be like that, okay? That's not you."

The gentle rebuke in Gus's voice calmed him just like it always did. "You're right. I'm overreacting. It's just…" He raked his sweaty hair away from his face with a deep sigh. "I never thought being with someone would make me feel this insecure."

"Talk to him, Rikky. Get everything out in the open and deal with it."

He drew his knees up, as if he could hide behind them. "I'm scared."

Her voice softened. "Of course you are. Laying yourself open like that is scary. But honey, it's the only way."

He thought of asking how she knew that, when her relationships with men up until now had been a few hours at a time, but decided against it. She dealt with people every day. He didn't. Plus, she was usually right about everything, so why not this?

"I guess so." He smiled at the phone. "Thanks, Gus."

"Any time. You know that." Someone spoke in the background. Gus answered. Henrik couldn't hear anything she said before she came back on the phone. "I need to go. Darryl and I are going to go get some dinner while I wait for my car. Will you be okay?"

"Yeah, I'm fine. Tell Darryl I said hi."

"I will. Love you."

"Love you too. Bye."

Henrik set his phone beside him on the chair and stared at the scrape on his knee from where he'd fallen in the woods yesterday during his run. Gus was right. As terrifying as he found the prospect of baring all his fears and insecurities to Marco, he needed to do it. Talking it all out was the best way to get rid of the tension between them and move forward.

The real question was, would they move on together, or apart?

Henrik wasn't sure he had the courage to learn the answer.

§ § §

Marco locked the shop's door twenty minutes late and turned the sign around to read *Closed*. "Thank fuck. What a day." He and Darryl had been running their asses off from the minute they opened that morning. They hadn't even had time to stop for lunch.

"You said it, boss." Behind the register, Darryl tucked the stack of twenties he'd just finished counting into the bank bag. "It was pretty awesome money-wise, though. We've got nearly a grand in cash here, and I haven't even added up the credit card receipts yet."

Marco let out a celebratory whoop, which Darryl echoed with a laugh. "Hell, yeah. That makes it all worthwhile, man."

"Right. Like you'd do anything else, even if you never made a dime."

"Point." Grinning, Marco strode over and rifled through

the credit card slips. The stack wasn't huge, but more than one showed four figures to the left of the decimal. "I like making money, though. Especially on days like this."

"No argument from me. You make money, I make money too."

"You make money no matter what," Marco pointed out. "You're an employee."

"Yeah, well, if you didn't make money you couldn't afford to keep me." Darryl took the receipts from Marco's hand. "Your big-ass sculptures are getting pretty popular lately."

Marco nodded, pride blooming inside him. "You have no idea how happy that makes me. I fucking *love* doing those. I'm glad they're selling." He glanced toward the one standing in the far corner—a sleek deer made of smoky dark gray glass, just translucent enough to make out a hint of the shelving behind the figure through its clean-lined body. "There's only the one left, though. I guess I'd better get busy making some more."

"Yeah, we could use more. They've been selling pretty steady lately." Fishing Marco's calculator out of the drawer under the counter, Darryl set it next to the register and started adding up the credit card slips. He glanced up at Marco with raised eyebrows. "Don't you want to go spend some time with Rikky, though? I mean, the shop's closed tomorrow, you could stay the night and relax for a little while."

Marco pressed his lips together to hold back a totally childish retort. Darryl was only trying to be nice. He didn't know anything about Marco's mixed feelings lately when it came to Rik. Hell, if he did he would've been even more annoyingly pushy about trying to get Marco back up the mountain.

If he could, Marco would've blamed it on Gus, but he knew better. Gus hadn't said a damn word about Marco's increasingly frequent use of the too-busy excuse to either not stay the night with Rik or not go up to see him at all in the last couple of weeks. Or at least, she hadn't said anything to *him*. He assumed she hadn't said anything to Darryl because Darryl couldn't keep a secret if the fate of the universe depended on it and if she'd said anything to him, he'd have told Marco in an earnest if misguided attempt to make him Do The Right Thing.

Kind of like he was doing now.

Marco frowned. "What's Gus been saying to you?"

Darryl's eyes widened. "Huh? What do you mean?"

Marco studied his assistant's face, every innocent, what-did-I-say line of it. Either he was very, very good, or he really didn't know what Marco was talking about.

Since Darryl and deceit had never been comfortable bedfellows, Marco was willing to bet on the latter.

"Never mind." Marco flashed his best fake smile, which—unlike Darryl's—was pretty damn convincing. He wasn't sure how he felt about that anymore. "July Fourth's kept me pretty busy. I'm planning to go see him tonight, though."

"Good." Darryl tapped on the calculator, shuffled through the slips, and kept his eyes on his work. "Rikky's a good guy."

Translation: Gus loves him, so I'm interested in his welfare.

Cynical, maybe, but Marco didn't think he was too far off the mark.

Or maybe he was. No one could meet Rik and *not* like him, as far as Marco was concerned. Besides which, Darryl tended to get along with almost everyone.

"He really is," Marco answered, half to himself. He laughed when Darryl shot him a cautious look. He supposed that's what he got for wandering too long in his private thoughts before resuming a conversation. "Okay, I'm gonna go shower real quick. Are you going up to see Gus? Need a ride?"

Darryl shook his head. "Gus is out of town. She had an in-person meeting today in New York with some of the veeps of her company."

"Oh. Okay." Gus was so down to earth—and, if he was honest, so young and gorgeous—that sometimes he forgot she ran a multi-national corporation. "Well, whenever you talk to her, tell her I said hello and give 'em hell."

Darryl laughed. "I'll do that." He paper-clipped the credit card slips together, put them in the bank bag, zipped and locked it. "I'll drop this off on my way out. See you tomorrow, Marco. Give Rikky my love."

"I will. Bye, brother." He slapped Darryl on the shoulder and headed into the back and up the stairs to his apartment over the shop.

In the shower, Marco thought about himself and Rik while he soaped off the stress of the day. How every time he'd been to the estate lately, Rik seemed on the verge of some huge revelation. How he'd become increasingly good at hiding his feelings behind his bright smile, his eager touch and the purity he radiated no matter how often Marco took him, or what sorts of things they did together in the privacy of Rik's bedroom. How all the things neither of them were saying hung between them like an invisible lead curtain, dulling every touch and leaching the meaning from every word they spoke to each other.

Mostly, Marco thought of how Rik's presence had become both necessary and troublesome to him. Troublesome, because he wasn't used to a relationship with a man who wouldn't talk to him and who he, apparently, couldn't bring himself to talk to either. It didn't make any sense. Marco had always been a straightforward man, in his love affairs even more than the rest of his life. He didn't like secrets and lies. So what made him hold his tongue, time and time again, when it came to dragging the truth out of Rik? What was he so afraid of?

If he was honest with himself, he knew his silence had more to do with himself than Henrik. With the knowledge that what he felt for Rik had become way too intense way too quickly. He wasn't sure he was ready for what that meant. Letting Rik think Marco was in this for the long haul wouldn't be fair, when Marco himself didn't know if he could do it.

On the other hand, he could no longer imagine his life without Rik in it.

Irritated with himself, Marco finished rinsing, turned off the water and snatched his towel off the rack. For now, he wouldn't think about it. He'd go up the mountain, spend the night making love to Rik and not let any poisonous thoughts sour it for either of them.

He could ignore the fact that not thinking about it was no longer an option.

For now.

§ § §

Henrik was in the library when Marco arrived, strolling in with his usual rakish smile and an overnight bag on his shoulder. "Hey, Rik. Sorry I'm late." He dropped the bag on the floor. "We were run off our feet today."

"Don't worry about it." Setting his book on the table beside him, Henrik jumped up, strode over to Marco and greeted him with an enthusiastic kiss. When the kiss ended, he pulled back to study Marco's face. "I'm glad you could make it tonight. I've missed you."

A look Henrik couldn't decipher slid through Marco's eyes. "I've missed you too. It's been *way* too long since I've been up the mountain."

"Only a few days." Henrik laughed when Marco arched an eyebrow at him. "Okay, yes. It's been too long."

"Damn right it has." Framing Henrik's face in his hands, Marco claimed another kiss, longer and deeper than the previous one. He pressed his body against Henrik's, one knee bending to trap Henrik's leg. "I want you to feel as frustrated by being apart as I do. I'm kind of a bastard that way."

The growl in Marco's voice matched the teasing tilt of his smile, but the look in his eyes was deadly serious. Irritated, yet not wanting to let go of Marco now that he was finally here, Henrik tightened his arms around Marco's waist. "You have no *idea* how frustrating it is to be stuck up here alone, not knowing when or if you'll be able to come up." Marco's back tensed beneath Henrik's hands. He clung, heart pounding. "I didn't want you to feel bad about that. I know you're busy. I know how important your art is to you. I would never take you away from that."

The last statement wasn't completely true. Certainly, Henrik had no desire to separate Marco from his art. It was a part of him, one of the many things that made him such a fascinating person. A small, selfish little part of him, however, wanted nothing more than to have Marco all to himself. To be the sole focus of Marco's attention, without the far more interesting world Outside—especially Furnace Glassworks and his creative domain—to lure him away.

Taking Henrik by the shoulders, Marco pushed him back enough to look at him. For several long, tense seconds, Marco stared into Henrik's eyes as if he could see inside his skull if only he tried hard enough. Finally, Marco dropped his hands with a sigh. "I didn't want to do this just yet. Hell, I didn't want to do it at all, if you want the truth. But I think it has to happen, and I think it needs to happen now."

Marco's face was as serious as Henrik had ever seen it. He thought he knew what that meant.

This is it. He's tired of me, and he's ending it.

Henrik's knees went weak. He stayed upright through sheer willpower, determined not to show his devastation to the man who'd gutted him. "That's fine with me. If you're going to break up with me, I'd rather you did it now instead of getting one more fuck first."

Okay, that little speech dripped with bitterness and heartbreak, but he couldn't help it. A man could only handle so much.

Marco's eyes went wide. "What? I'm not breaking up with you."

"You're not?"

"No. Where in the hell did you get that idea?"

"I...well..." Henrik laughed, lightheaded with a mix of relief and confusion. "I don't know. You looked so serious, and it seemed like you've been staying away a lot lately—although I completely understand that, like I said before—and I just thought—"

"You jumped to conclusions. But I can see that, I guess." Marco took both of Henrik's hands into his. "The fact that you did that just proves to me that I'm right, though."

"About what?" Henrik laced his fingers through Marco's. The solemn expression on Marco's face still scared him, even if it didn't mean they were breaking up. "What do you think needs to happen?"

"Nothing so terrible, but something we probably should've done a long time ago." Marco's mouth hitched into a wry smile. "We need to talk."

Chapter Ten

Apprehension curdled in the pit of Henrik's stomach. He ignored the temptation to pretend ignorance regarding the subject of this discussion and nodded instead. "You're right. Come on, I'll pour us a drink."

Henrik dropped one of Marco's hands but kept hold of the other one as they left the library. The physical contact comforted him. Gave him hope that maybe Marco wouldn't change his mind about breaking up once he'd seen all Henrik's fears, weaknesses and insecurities laid bare.

In the cozy den at the rear of the house off the breakfast nook, Marco settled on the brown leather sofa beside the picture window while Henrik went to pour them each a whiskey and soda from the bar.

Neither said a word until Henrik sat beside Marco and handed him his glass. Marco took it with a smile that seemed nervous. "Thanks."

"Sure."

Silence fell again. Marco opened his mouth, then shut it again. A deep furrow dug into his brow. He turned to stare out the window.

Henrik sipped his whiskey. His insides churned with rising anxiety. All this time, he'd dreaded having his innermost thoughts and feelings opened up for Marco's inspection, because if Marco knew the extent of Henrik's doubts—both of himself and of Marco—he'd surely lose interest. Watching Marco's face, though, Henrik wondered if he shouldn't be more afraid of whatever was going on in Marco's head *now*.

"I never met anybody quite like you," Marco said, his gaze still fixed on the forested slopes cloaked in dusk outside. "I mean, let's face it, people lie. They hide things. Everybody does it. But not you. When I first met you, it was like you weren't even *capable* of hiding anything." He turned to look at Henrik, finally, his eyes alight with a complex brew of affection, admiration and sorrow. "I admired that about you. It was the number one thing that attracted me to you."

Admired. Was. Like it was all in the past.

Henrik felt cold inside. He gulped whiskey, hoping it would steady his voice. "Yeah, you've said. Sounds like that's changed."

Putting his glass on the coffee table, Marco scooted closer and rested a hand on Henrik's bare knee. "I feel like I hardly know you anymore. Like I can't trust what I'm seeing on your face. Maybe that shouldn't bother me, but it does."

For the first time, Marco's nearness made Henrik feel claustrophobic. He rose, skirted the end of the sofa and stood in front of another of the room's huge windows to peer out into the deepening dark. "Maybe I don't like being such an open book. Maybe I'd like to keep my thoughts to myself until I choose to share them, like we both agreed I have a right to do." He took another drink. It was starting to go to his head. "I can't tell what you're thinking or feeling just by looking at you. Why is that fine for you, but not for me?"

Silence. Henrik clutched his glass tighter and wished he had the courage to look at Marco.

The leather rustled. From the corner of his eye, Henrik saw Marco pick up his drink and toss back most of it, then slump against the cushions and stare at the ceiling. "I'm not trying to make you tell me things you're not comfortable talking about. I'm not even trying to…" He waved a hand in the air, as if he could conjure what he was trying to say into physical form. "I don't know. Make you go back to how you used to be, or whatever. People change. That's life. Either you deal with it, or you live off the grid and learn to love your own company."

Frustrated, confused and hot inside with a growing indignation, Henrik turned to face Marco. "Then I don't understand. If you're magnanimous enough to accept the new me—"

"Oh, for fuck's sake." Marco plunked his glass down again,

stood and shoved both hands in his back pockets. "You know, it's really hard to have an honest conversation if you're going to be sarcastic."

Henrik wanted to deny it, but that would be childish. He was beginning to see now where the work came into a relationship. Swallowing your pride, your hurt feelings and the urge to lash out in favor of a calm, rational discussion wasn't nearly as easy as he'd always imagined.

"Fair enough." Henrik took a couple of steps closer to the sofa, but didn't sit. He still felt crowded, which was a first in his own house. He resented Marco for that. "I still don't understand, though. You just said that people change, and it's something everyone has to deal with. You say I've changed, but you also say that change bothers you, and that's what I don't get. Does it bother you that you actually have to ask what I'm thinking now? Or does it bother you that I might not tell you?"

"Both." Marco had the gall to glare. "Look, I'm not proud of it. But we can't get past any of this until we get it out there in the open and talk it out. And that goes double for the ugly stuff."

Henrik let out a sharp laugh. "Well, at least you can admit that it's ugly."

"Goddammit." Marco rubbed both hands over his face. When he dropped them, the glare was gone. He looked tired and defeated. "Yeah, it's not pretty. But I can't help how I feel. I just want to be honest with you about it. The only thing I expect of you is to be honest with me, too. I don't want to *make* you tell me stuff. But if you say something to me, I want it to be the truth." He sank onto the sofa, his head down. "I don't think that's too much to ask."

He was right, and Henrik knew it. Which did nothing to ease the near-panic pushing his pulse into a nausea-inducing gallop.

Moving with deliberate care since his hands shook, Henrik set his glass on the table, sat down beside Marco and took his hand. "I'm scared."

Marco moved closer. He wove his fingers through Henrik's,

holding tight. "Scared of what?"

The words caught in Henrik's throat. He leaned against Marco for strength and forced himself to speak anyway. "I've never been with a man before you, Marco. I don't know anything about the world except what I've learned online. I can't even leave this estate. I probably never will." He stared at the plush burgundy rug beneath his feet. "Most people would say that's pretty high maintenance."

He couldn't bring himself to express his fears more directly, but Marco was a smart man. He laid his free hand on Henrik's cheek and turned his head until he was looking into Marco's eyes. "I won't pretend any of this is easy, Rik. It's not, and we both know that. But I want to try. I think you're worth it."

The certainty in Marco's words eased some of the anxiety that had been gnawing at Henrik's gut lately. He squeezed Marco's hand. "I don't know what I'm doing, but I want to try too."

"Good." Marco leaned in for a quick, soft kiss. "Nobody ever really knows what they're doing when it comes to relationships. But we're in this thing together. As long as we're honest with each other, we'll be fine."

"Okay." Henrik smiled, feeling more relaxed by the second. "I'm glad we talked. You were right. It was good to get this stuff out in the open."

Marco peered at him, dark eyes full of something that made Henrik's breath come short. For a moment, Henrik knew—he *knew*—Marco was about to say something. His throat went dry, his chest tight. He didn't know whether to label the feeling anticipation or terror.

When Marco kissed him again instead of speaking, Henrik couldn't help the relief that washed through him along with the usual rush of desire.

Nor could he help the doubt still lingering in a dark little corner of his heart.

§ § §

In the first few days after the big talk with Rik, Marco bit the bullet and made himself a schedule of days in the hot shop and days to go up the mountain. He'd always hated schedules, but he had to admit that knowing where he was going to be ahead of time not only made Rik feel more secure, but actually improved Marco's creative output. With his best work to date selling as fast as he could produce it and a man who made him happier than he'd thought possible, Marco spent the rest of July feeling as though he'd fallen into an alternate universe.

Every day, he patted himself on the back for deciding to stick it out with Rik. He hadn't been sure he would until Rik held his hand and admitted in that soft, slightly sad voice that he was scared of Marco leaving him. The fact that the confession made Marco feel needed rather than smothered had erased all doubt from his mind, and he'd promised Rik they'd stay together.

He didn't start second guessing himself until the first days of August.

It would've been nice if he could blame his growing uneasiness on Henrik. God knew he tried. But the fault lay squarely on his own shoulders, and he couldn't pretend otherwise.

The question was, what to do about it?

The shop's back door squealed open, startling him out of his thoughts. "Morning, Darryl," he called without looking. "There's coffee in the office, if you want some." He gestured with his own mug.

"Awesome. Thanks." Darryl came into view, looking way too perky for a Monday. He held up a paper bag. "I stopped for bagels on the way. Looks like between us, we made breakfast."

Marco's stomach rumbled, reminding him he hadn't eaten since lunch yesterday. That's what happened when he got caught up in the hot shop. He laughed in spite of his morose mood. "We make a great team."

"Hell, yeah." Darryl set the bag on the counter. "Coffee time. Be right back."

Marco took a whole oats bagel out of the bag and cut it in

half. He was smearing it with a liberal helping of honey nut cream cheese when Darryl returned, coffee mug in hand and a determined expression on his face.

Picking up half of his bagel, Marco took a big bite. He watched Darryl while he chewed. "What're you looking at me like that for?"

"No reason." Darryl glanced at Marco with the sly sideways look that meant he was up to something. He fished an everything bagel out of the bag, cut it and spread on a nearly invisible layer of vegetable cream cheese. "How's Rikky? I haven't seen him for a while."

Ah. So that was Darryl's game. Find out what was up between Marco and Rik.

Busybody.

Marco studied Darryl with well-deserved suspicion, the nosy bastard. "He's fine. Saw him Saturday night." He grinned, struck by a sudden fit of mischief. "We did this thing where—"

"Okay, stop." Darryl pointed a half-eaten hunk of bagel in Marco's face. "I swear to God, one more word and I'll go into all kinds of nasty detail about that thing I do that makes Gus go *aaaaah, baaaaaby*!"

The mental image—plus Darryl's hilariously high-pitched imitation of Gus's voice—made Marco laugh and groan at the same time. "Shit. I'd threaten to tell her you said that, only I don't really want her to kill you."

Darryl waved his bagel in a gesture of supreme unconcern. "Hell, man, she wouldn't. You can't embarrass her. She's way too self-confident. Woman could walk into a board meeting bare-ass naked and make everybody else feel like *they're* the ones who look stupid." A love-struck grin spread over his face. "I'm telling you, there's nobody on earth like her."

"I can tell." Marco bit into his bagel again. "I've never seen you like this before."

Darryl shrugged. "I'm in love. Never been in love before, but

I like it."

"Wow." Marco cupped his coffee mug in both hands and sipped, trying not to look as shocked as he felt. "Does Gus know?"

"I haven't told her yet. But it'll be soon." Darryl smiled, his expression serene. "She loves me, too. I can tell. So it's all good."

Just like that, Marco's previous dark mood settled over him again like a storm cloud, though he wasn't sure why. He smiled wide in an attempt to hide it. "Cool. As long as you're happy, I'm happy for you."

"Yeah. Thanks." Tearing off a piece of bagel, Darryl popped it into his mouth and chewed, studying Marco with a gaze too keen for comfort. "What's up?"

Taken aback, Marco stared. "Huh? What do you mean?"

"When I first came in, you were thinking pretty hard about something. Then we started talking, and you seemed fine. Now all of a sudden you get this look like your favorite aunt died." Darryl picked up his coffee and took a sip, still watching Marco's face. "So what gives?"

Marco sighed. He really didn't want to talk about this, especially since he couldn't put his concerns into words, even in his head. "I don't know. Look, I don't mean to be a dick, but I'm not sure what's wrong, exactly, and I feel weird talking about it when I can't even figure out what I'm thinking." He hunched over his coffee mug, feeling miserable and a lot like a dick no matter how much he didn't want to be. "Sorry."

"Naw, come on. You know you can talk to me any time you want, but you don't *have* to." Darryl clasped his shoulder. "Tell you what, though. Whatever's eating you, you better not hide it from Rikky."

"I know." Marco did his best to squash the automatic surge of irritation. After all, Darryl was arguably—okay, no, *definitely*—his best friend in the world other than Rik, and he was only trying to help.

Moved by a sudden overflow of affection, Marco let go of his coffee mug and hugged Darryl hard, ignoring his surprised squeak. "Thanks, man."

If Darryl wondered what the hell had gotten into Marco, he hid it well. He returned the hug, slapping Marco's back. "Hey, we're brothers, right? Brothers gotta look out for each other."

"Fuck, yeah." Marco drew back, his best hiding-everything smile on his face. "Okay. Well. Guess we better get busy. Almost time to open."

"Yeah." Darryl held onto Marco's wrist. His gaze bored into Marco's skull. "Listen, I know it's not on this schedule thing of yours, but you can go up the mountain tonight if you want. Gus texted me last night, she said she's got an emergency board meeting tonight so she can't come to town like she'd planned."

A month ago, Marco would've gone. Eagerly.

Now? He couldn't deny the fact that he'd rather work in the hot shop like he'd planned. Not because Rik had drifted back into secrecy, even though he had, to some extent. No, he wanted the night to himself because the depth of his feelings for Rik terrified him right down to his marrow, and he had no idea how to deal with it.

He put on his best casual expression. "I would, but I really need to work in the hot shop today. Especially with how fast my stuff's been selling lately. Which is awesome, by the way, and at least partly down to your salesman skill, so thanks for that." He lifted his mug in a toast.

Darryl's eyes narrowed. "Marco, are you sure you're okay?"

"I'm fine. Honest." Uncomfortable with Darryl's dagger-sharp stare, Marco took his coffee and the remainder of his bagel and headed for the office. "I'm going to check a couple of things with the books. I'll be back out before we open."

"Okay. Sure."

Marco heard the scoff in Darryl's voice, but ignored it. He had more important things to think about. Like how he didn't know if he could reconcile his feelings for Rik with the sacrifices it would take to truly commit to him.

Inside, Marco knew it was too late for doubts. His heart had already committed itself, whether his brain liked it or not. The only thing left to think about was how to make it all work, for both of them.

He sighed. Looked like he and Rik had another serious conversation in their mutual future. And damned if he didn't look forward to this one even less than the last one.

He'd barely brought up the shop's financial records on the office computer when the phone out in the shop rang. He heard Darryl answer it. A moment later, his office phone beeped. The number out front showed on the display.

Wrinkling his nose, he picked it up. "I'm busy. Can't whoever it is wait? Or deal with you instead?"

"That's what I told her," Darryl said. "Only I said it nicer than that, of course."

Marco rolled his eyes. "That's why I make you answer the phone."

"No shit. Anyway, she said it was personal and she had to talk to you directly."

"Jesus. Fine. Who is it?" Marco rubbed at the pain starting in his temple. If he had to talk to one more rich snob who thought their commission was more important than everyone else's, he thought he might go postal.

"She wouldn't give me a last name." Darryl sounded pretty put out about that. "Said just to tell you it's Bonnie."

Marco stared, shocked. He only knew one Bonnie. He'd never expected to talk to her again after their last fight, when she called him a traitor to his family for choosing to be true to himself instead of pretending he could be happy with an office job and a wife, and he told her to fuck off and die.

Eight years. Hell, almost nine now. He'd been a kid then, barely in his twenties, full of himself and angry at the world. She hadn't been a whole lot better.

But she'd called. Knowing he was still a glass artist-slash-sculptor instead of a cubicle dweller. Knowing he was even further out of the closet than he'd been back then. She'd still called. He seriously doubted she'd tracked him down and contacted him just to dig the knife deeper.

Which meant he should probably talk to her instead of telling Darryl to tell her to fuck off and leave him alone. Not that Darryl would say such a thing to anyone, ever.

"Marco? Should I put her through?"

Christ, he hoped he didn't regret this later. "Yeah, put her through."

"You got it."

The phone clicked when Darryl switched back to the other line. Marco ran a hand over his newly-shorn head. He was nervous, which pissed him off, but he didn't know what he was supposed to do about it.

Another click sounded in his ear as Darryl put Bonnie through. Marco cleared his throat, squared his shoulders and steeled himself to speak in a civil tone. "Hey, sis."

Chapter Eleven

Henrik was vacuuming one of the guest suites on the second floor in preparation for Gus's upcoming corporate retreat when he got Marco's text canceling on him for the weekend. He barely managed to force a terse acknowledgement from his shaking fingers before throwing his phone onto the plush guest bed. It didn't give quite the same satisfaction as smashing something, but it was better than nothing. He was still half-afraid his grandfather would know if he broke any of the valuable objects in the guest room.

"Fuck!" He sat on the floor and dropped his head into his hands. "Dammit, Marco. You fucking bastard."

"Rikky?" Gus, who'd been cleaning the suite next door, stuck her head around the door frame. "Oh my God. Are you all right?" She hurried over and crouched beside Henrik, one cool palm on his back and the other hand gently prying his fingers away from his face. "What happened?"

He met her gaze, knowing he looked as furious and devastated as he felt. "Marco canceled."

Gus's mouth made a silent *Oh*. Her expression softened in sympathy edged with guilt. She knew exactly what this weekend had meant to Henrik. The corporate retreats only happened once a year, but he hated them. He usually spent the weekend hiding in his room with the TV turned up loud to drown out the voices. For the last couple of years, he'd leaned heavily on Xanax as well during those weekends, since his psychiatrist had started letting him take the drug for anxiety again.

For a while, with Marco, he'd thought he wouldn't need it anymore, not even for corporate retreat weekend. Marco had said he'd come over and stay with Henrik all weekend, from Friday night to Monday morning, to help him get through what was, for Henrik, the worst three days of the year. Henrik had snatched at the offer like the lifeline it was. And now Marco had canceled.

Let down didn't quite cover how Henrik felt. Betrayed came closer.

Settling on the floor beside Henrik, Gus slipped an arm around his shoulders. "I'm sorry, honey. Did he say why?"

"His sister and her family arrived in town unexpectedly." Henrik laughed. It sounded bitter. "I didn't even know he had a sister."

"Oh. Well, apparently they haven't spoken to each other in quite a few years. Marco's been on the outs with his family for a long time."

Henrik stared at Gus, who was frowning at the carpet. "How do *you* know all that?"

"Darryl, of course." She gave him a crooked smile, looking impish and sad at the same time. "He loves Marco like a brother, he's a mother hen at heart, and he is incapable of keeping anything to himself. Which means I've learned a lot more about Marco than I ever wanted to know." She bit her lip. "Darryl actually mentioned Marco's sister the other day when I saw him. Apparently Bonnie—the sister—called on Monday and wanted to see Marco. She's gotten married and started a family since the last time they spoke, and she felt it was time they reconciled."

Monday. Three days ago. Not that he and Marco had actually seen each other in that time, but it wasn't like Marco couldn't call, or email. They could even video chat. In fact, they'd had a text chat last night. Marco could've said something then, but he hadn't. That hurt more than Henrik would've thought possible.

"Great. Mr. Honest waxes eloquent about how we need to tell each other everything, then I have to find out important things about him from you by way of Darryl." Henrik shook his head. His throat ached with the complex tangle of emotion trying to shove its way out. "I don't even know how to be without him anymore, but I can't help feeling like he's pulling away from me. I don't know what to do."

"Oh, sweetheart." Gus circled his chest with both arms and curled close, her head pressed against his. "Don't give up.

Whatever you do, *don't* give up. I think this whole relationship scares him as much as it scares you, but I also think he wants it just as much as you do. His family isn't going to take him away from you. The only people who can break you up are you and him."

"But they're more important to him right now," he whispered, putting what he most feared into words. "And who can blame him? That's always going to happen. There's always going to be someone or something more important than me. How can it ever be any other way, when it's so easy to just leave me up here on my mountain and forget about me?" Gus lifted her head, and he peered at her as if she might actually have the answer to his dilemma, though he knew she didn't. "He's the center of my whole life now, Gus. I know it's selfish, but I want to be that to him, too, and I just don't see how that can ever happen."

Gus watched him with sympathy in her eyes. "I don't know what's going to happen. I wish I could say I do. But don't sell Marco short. He cares a lot about you. I can't imagine he would ever just leave you up here and forget about you, no matter what else is going on in his life."

Henrik hadn't yet told her about all the times over the last few weeks that Marco had planned to come up the mountain and canceled for one reason or another, and he found he didn't have the heart to tell her now. Instead, he managed a nod and an anemic smile. "You're right, of course. You're always right."

Her forehead furrowed as if she couldn't decide whether or not he meant it. She kept any suspicions to herself, though, probably because she had an enormous amount of work to do before the veeps and the board arrived tomorrow. She smiled. "Of course I am." Tightening her grip on him, she planted a kiss on his cheek, then let him go and rose to her feet. "I guess I should finish the other room, then I need to go over the financial dashboards and make sure my presentation is ready to go."

Henrik stood alongside her. "You should let me finish the cleaning. It's not like I have anything else I need to do."

"Just let me finish up the one suite. I need a break from

staring at computer screens." She clasped her hands in front of her. "Please."

He laughed in spite of the cold pain gnawing at his gut. "Like I could tell you what to do anyway. Go on."

Grasping his hand, she gave it a squeeze. "Rikky. Promise me you'll come find me and talk to me if you need me, okay? Any time, no matter what else is going on. Promise."

"I will," he said, though he had no intention of interrupting her retreat for any of his silly romantic difficulties. He let go of her hand and gave her a playful shove. "Now get going. I know how much you have to do."

"This is true. But I always have time for the most important person in my life." She left the room with a smile.

Henrik went back to his vacuuming, his thoughts turning to Marco again. He knew Gus meant what she said. She was there for him if he needed her. She'd always been there for him, all their lives. He was incredibly grateful to her for that. But this weekend was important to her, and to the company. The last thing he wanted to do right now was tie her down with more of his problems.

Besides, a glimmer of an idea had sparked in the back of Henrik's mind and begun to grow. An idea that would prove to Marco that being with Henrik didn't have to mean being shut away from the world.

If he could pull it off. And that was a big if.

"You have to," he mumbled, lifting the heavy cotton bed skirt to vacuum as far under the king-plus bed as he could get. "No choice."

No choice. Not if he wanted to move forward with Marco.

The thought of what he planned to do made his heart thud painfully hard. It was time—past time—he took this step, though. For himself as much as for Marco.

Nothing had ever scared him the way this did. But he was determined. Being with Marco had shown him an inner strength he never knew he had. This latest development simply gave him the push he needed to do what he already knew in his heart needed to be done.

"You can do it," he whispered, the sound drowned in the hum of the vacuum.

For the first time in eight years, he believed it.

§ § §

Reconciling with his sister after almost nine years with no contact wasn't nearly as painful as Marco had feared.

Which wasn't to say it was all wine and roses. But, yeah, they ended up getting along pretty well.

Maybe age had mellowed them. Hell, Marco knew it had mellowed *him*, at least.

"Hey, Marco." The voice with its faint French accent jostled him out of his thoughts. Across the table, the brother-in-law he'd just met yesterday flashed his friendly smile. "What are you thinking?"

"Nothing much." Marco smiled back. He didn't even have to fake it, for a wonder. Pierre—good God, his sister had married a *Pierre*—might not be the sharpest crayon in the box, but he was a nice guy, and from what Marco could tell a great husband and dad. "Just kind of wishing me and Bonnie hadn't wasted so many years not talking, you know?"

Pierre nodded. "At least you're talking now. And I'm very glad. I never had a brother. I like it."

"Yeah, me too. I only ever had a sister, and you know what she's like." Marco grinned when Pierre laughed.

When Bonnie introduced Marco to her husband the previous morning—their first opportunity to get together—Marco had braced himself for the inevitable coolness he got from people who knew ahead of time he was gay, didn't approve but weren't allowed to say anything about it. What he'd gotten instead was a warm smile, a crushing hug and a genuine sense of welcome. It was a nice change of pace.

"All right, what're the two of you laughing at?" Bonnie returned from the bathroom with two-year-old Vincent on her hip and five-year-old Cherie trailing behind, singing something she'd apparently made up on the drive over. Settling Vincent into her husband's outstretched arms, Bonnie nudged Cherie into the seat beside Marco then sat beside her. "Men laughing at stuff is never good."

"No, love." Pierre cuddled Vincent against his chest. The toddler promptly laid his curly brown head against his dad's shoulder and shut his eyes. "I was just telling Marco how happy I am to have a brother."

"And I was just agreeing." Marco slid the basket of tortilla chips—what was left of them—in range of Cherie's reaching hand. "There you go, sweetie. You like those, huh?"

She nodded, little black ponytails bobbing, grabbed the biggest chip she could find and bit off a chunk. She peered up at him with solemn brown eyes. "Mama says you like boys instead of girls."

Marco blinked. Beside him, Bonnie groaned. "Cherie, honey, you shouldn't—"

"No, it's okay. There's no reason she can't ask if she wants to know." Marco smiled at his little niece, who had begun to look as though she thought she was in trouble. "Yeah, I like boys."

Cherie crunched her chip, her round face thoughtful. "Like getting married?"

In fact, he'd never considered getting married, even if he was allowed to, but he wasn't about to attempt that conversation with a five year old. Especially when he knew what she meant. He nodded. "Yeah. Like getting married."

She finished her chip and reached for another, studying him with unusual intensity for such a youngster. "Okay." Having given her approval, she folded her knees under her and stretched her arm towards the half-empty cup of salsa on the other side of the table. "Want sauce. Please?"

Laughing, Pierre slid the salsa to where Cherie could reach it.

"Well. All right, then."

"Indeed. The princess has spoken." Bonnie rested an elbow on the table and looked at Marco. "So, since Miss Priss has broken the ice, are you seeing anyone?"

Marco's stomach rolled, making him wish he'd gotten the gazpacho for dinner instead of the grande burrito. He wasn't ashamed of Rik. On the other hand, he had no idea how to explain Rik to the sister with whom he'd barely become reacquainted and the brother-in-law he'd only just met. Never mind trying to couch the whole thing in words appropriate for the first-grade-and-under set.

He took a good long drink of his beer to give himself a few seconds to think. "Well, yeah, I am."

Bonnie's eyes lit up with the gossip-gleam he remembered from high school. "That's great! Tell us about him." She touched his arm, as if she'd realized that maybe she was being nosy. "If that's okay. I don't mean to push you. I'm just interested, that's all."

Marco couldn't help chuckling. This was a far different Bonnie than the one he'd grown up with. The years *had* changed her, just as they'd changed him. "He lives up the mountain, about an hour outside town. His name's Henrik Schweitzer. He's…" God, what to say, that wouldn't make him sound like a gushing girl? "He's one of a kind. Just a wonderful guy."

Bonnie's expression turned dreamy and starry-eyed. Before she could ask anything he wouldn't want to answer, Pierre sat up straighter, his eyes wide. "Wait, is this Henrik Schweitzer of Schweitzer International? The mineral trading company?"

To his embarrassment, Marco had to think hard for a moment before he remembered. Henrik rarely talked about his business, and Marco had only heard Gus mention the title a couple of times. "Yeah, it is. You're familiar with the business?"

"Yes, indeed. The company where I work manufactures computer components. We deal with Schweitzer all the time. They're an excellent company, especially since old Otto

Schweitzer retired and turned over the business to his grandson. Which would be Henrik." Pierre leaned forward, little Vincent dozing on his shoulder and barely contained excitement written all over his face. "You're dating a multi-millionaire, Marco."

Marco was surprised Pierre didn't know that Gus was the one running the company. He'd gotten the idea that everyone knew. If that wasn't the case though, he figured it wasn't up to him to let the cat out of the bag.

He grinned at his brother-in-law. "I know. You wouldn't know it if you hung out with him, though. He's very down to earth."

"That's wonderful. I'm so glad you've found someone who makes you happy. And I guess it doesn't hurt that he's rich." Bonnie laid her hand on Marco's arm again while Pierre laughed, making Vincent squirm and grumble. "We'd love to meet him, if he can get away while we're here."

What to say? Marco wasn't ashamed of seeing an agoraphobic—or so he kept telling himself—but he didn't know if it was really his place to tell Rik's story. Not even to family.

"I'll ask, but I'm not sure. He and his cousin have a corporate retreat going on at their estate this weekend." There. That was the truth, even if it wasn't the reason why Rik couldn't come down the mountain.

"Oh. That's too bad."

Bonnie glanced at Pierre. They both looked disappointed, and Marco felt a twinge of guilt. It was for the best, though. He couldn't very well bring his family up to the estate uninvited this weekend of all times. He had no idea how Rik would react, even if he knew ahead of time they were coming. Marco didn't want to risk causing a panic attack.

Rik coming down the mountain? Yeah, that was out of the question.

"I'm sure he'd love to meet you." Marco smiled, well aware that his sister wouldn't notice that he was hiding anything since she didn't really know him anymore. "Maybe we can go up there next time you come for a visit. The kids would love his estate. He has a great pool."

Cherie, who'd gone back to her chips and her made-up song, abandoned both in favor of staring round-eyed at Marco. "I wanna swim in the pool! Can we?"

Across the table, the magic word cut through Vincent's semi-nap enough to make him twist around in his father's arms. "Poo!" he shouted at the top of his voice, drawing both frowns and grins from all over their section of the restaurant. "Fwim a poo!"

Marco laughed along with his sister and brother-in-law. He'd never wanted kids of his own, but he could get used to having a niece and nephew. These two were cute. "Sorry, guys, but we can't go swim in Rik's pool right now. He has really important company, so we can't go visit."

"We can swim in the hotel pool when we get back," Pierre said before Cherie could start using what Marco suspected were considerable persuasive skills on him. "Right now we're visiting with Uncle Marco."

"Ung Armo!" Vincent crowed, then dissolved into giggles for no discernible reason.

"Oh, my God," Bonnie groaned. "Sorry, Marco. Vinnie likes to yell everything right now."

"Hey, at least he's happy." Marco winked at Vincent, who found that hilarious. The little boy's full-throated laughter was infectious, and Marco ended up laughing along with him.

For some reason, the whole scene—mom, dad, kids, himself happily in the middle of it—made him miss Rik with a surprising fierceness. He didn't know why now, in particular. He always missed Rik when they were apart, but right now, the longing to hold Rik, to touch him, even to simply hear his voice, pulled at Marco's gut so hard it hurt.

The decision was made before he consciously realized it. He reached over to touch Bonnie's hand. "Could you let me out? I need to run outside and make a call real quick. Cell reception's sh— um, not so good in here."

Bonnie raised her eyebrows as if she knew exactly what he was doing, but she scooted out of the booth anyway, taking Cherie with her. Marco slid out, doing his best to ignore the knowing looks from Bonnie and Pierre, and strode toward the exit.

Outside, he plucked his sunglasses off the collar of his shirt and put them on. Six o'clock in late August in the mountains meant about three hours to go before dark, and the sun's rays beat down with fearsome force. Fishing his phone out of his jeans pocket, he hit the speed dial for Rik's number.

It rang six times, which was weird. Rik never let it go more than three unless he was sleeping or out running, and that never happened this time of day. In any case, he'd have it on voice mail if he couldn't answer.

Finally, the ringing stopped. "Hello?"

The voice wasn't Rik's.

Chapter Twelve

Instantly, adrenaline shot through Marco's blood. "You're not Rik. Who're you?"

"This is Dan Harrison. I'm a fireman."

Oh, God. Marco leaned against the wall, his knees weak and his heart hammering. "What's wrong? Where's Rik? Why're you answering his phone?"

"A taxi driver brought him to us. The driver said he'd given her an address to go to, but then he started panicking and having trouble breathing not long after they got into town, so she brought him here since we were closer than the hospital or urgent care."

Marco thought he might be sick. He slid down to the ground, ignoring all the alarmed looks from strangers passing by. "Are you taking him to the hospital? I can meet you there."

There was a short pause before the fireman spoke again. "Sorry, sir, but who are you?"

"Rik and I are…good friends. My name's Marco Ravél."

"Oh. Okay." Dan sounded relieved. "He asked for you, actually. Said he was coming into town to see you."

God, Rik. What in the hell did you do? Marco shut his eyes. "Please. Tell me if he's okay and what you're going to do."

"It seems as though he's suffered a panic attack. He said he had a history. We wanted to take him to the ED, but he refused, and he'd calmed down enough by that time that we really couldn't justify forcing him."

Rik's logic made sense to Marco. A crowded emergency room would've sent him into catatonia.

Fuck. Marco opened his eyes. The need to get to Rik drove him to his feet before he knew where he was going. "I'll come get him. Where are you?"

"The station in town. You know where it is?"

"Yeah, I know it. I'll be there in five minutes."

He cut off the call before Fireman Dan could say another word. If they didn't want him to come get Rik, that was just too fucking bad. He was going anyway.

§ § §

He should've known Bonnie wouldn't want to stay behind. Even when they were kids, she'd never been happy on the sidelines.

"I'm a nurse," she reminded him when he was forced to admit he was going to the fire station to pick up his boyfriend, though he'd hedged when it came to the reason Rik was there. "Maybe I can help."

"Maybe." He had to admit she probably knew her stuff when it came to problems like Rik's. She'd started out in psych nursing years ago, before she and Marco had their falling out, though she'd worked as an insurance case manager for the last few years. Still… "But, look, there's…well, extenuating circumstances."

Pierre's eyebrows went up. Cherie ignored them, too busy leaning on the table singing to her baby brother, who was doing his best to sing with her.

Bonnie's worried gaze didn't waver from Marco's face. "Like what?" She grasped his arm. "Marco, I know it's been a long time and I have to earn your trust again. But I feel like something bad might be happening here, and I'd like to help you if I can."

Marco tried to think of something to say that would sound reasonable without giving away all Rik's secrets. Nothing came to mind, and he didn't have time to stand there any longer.

Making the best decision he could, all things considered, he gave his sister a terse nod. "All right. You can come with me in my car." He glanced at Pierre. "Just Bonnie. Sorry, man. I promise I have a good reason."

Pierre nodded. "I understand. Go on."

Marco stood and chafed with impatience while Bonnie lifted

Cherie out of the way, slid out of her seat, gave Pierre a kiss and promised to call if she needed him to come pick her up. Finally, she shouldered her purse and followed Marco out the door.

The drive to the fire station seemed to take forever, even though it was less than four miles from the restaurant. Marco gripped the steering wheel hard and cursed under his breath as the typically heavy Gatlinburg traffic crawled forward at a painfully slow pace.

When they finally reached the station, Marco stopped the car, jumped out and ran for the station door without waiting for Bonnie. He heard her door open and close and the sound of her sandals slapping the pavement behind him as he jogged up to the open bay of the station.

A woman in a black T-shirt and jeans stood from the chair where she'd been sitting. "Hey. Are you Marco?"

"Yes." He looked around, but couldn't see anything but the two fire engines. "Where's Rik? Is he okay?"

"He will be." She glanced at Bonnie, standing quietly beside Marco. "I have to tell you, I'm not sure he was entirely happy about you coming to get him, but he agreed since there wasn't much choice. The taxi driver wasn't about to take him back home." The firefighter started toward the rear of the bay and gestured for Marco and Bonnie to follow. "He's in the back. Come on."

Marco followed her. Bonnie trailed behind him. The woman led them into a combined living room, dining room and kitchen in the back of the station. "Dan!" she called. "Henrik's friend is here."

"Great, thanks," a male voice answered from an open door on the far side of the room.

A tall, dark-haired man who looked like he belonged on one of those fireman calendars strolled into the room. Marco barely gave him a glance, though, because Rik sat huddled sideways in a green vinyl chair, his knees curled up tight against his chest and his face white. He didn't seem to notice Marco, but at least he was calm.

Marco went straight to him, knelt beside the chair and touched Rik's cheek. "Rik? It's me, Marco."

Rik blinked. His eyes focused on Marco, and his blank mask gave way to agony. "God, I'm sorry. I'm so sorry." He curled forward, covering his face with his hands.

Marco's heart broke. He rose and squeezed himself between Rik's back and the arm of the chair, and pulled Rik close. "Babe, no. Don't do that." He stroked Rik's hair away from his face. The fine blond strands were damp with sweat. Aching inside for Rik, Marco kissed the curve of Rik's neck. "You don't need to be sorry. All I care about is that you're all right."

For a few seconds, Rik didn't answer, just sat there shaking in Marco's arms. Finally, he relaxed enough to lean back against Marco's chest. "I'm okay." His voice emerged in a rough whisper. He turned enough to settle more firmly into Marco's embrace. "I wanted to come see you. Get away from the estate and just be with you instead. I…I thought I could do it." He grasped Marco's arm in an iron grip. His voice dropped so low Marco could barely hear him. "I was jealous that you were with your family instead of me. So stupid, fuck, I acted so stupid and so *selfish*, and now I'm keeping you from spending time with your family. I'm sorry."

Hearing Rik say those things hurt like a physical pain. Marco tilted Rik's face up and kissed him, aware of the awkward, uncomfortable silence around him and not giving a damn. "I told you, there's nothing to be sorry about. I shouldn't've canceled on you, not when I knew how much you needed me with you this weekend."

"Hang on a minute." Bonnie, who until then had been as silent as the crowd of firefighters gathered around watching the drama, stood at the far side of the chair and frowned at Marco, her arms crossed over her chest. "Marco, did you cancel your plans this weekend for us?"

Marco's cheeks heated. "You have a way of making it sound even worse."

She rolled her eyes. "Well, I happen to think it's pretty bad. I mean, I'm glad we got to see each other again after all these years, but honey, you're my *brother.* I would've worked with your schedule. We're here for several days."

"Yeah, I get it." Marco sighed and pressed his cheek to Rik's hair. "Twenty-twenty hindsight."

Bonnie glanced over at Fireman Dan, who was standing off to the side looking stunned. "Dan, is Henrik okay physically?"

"Seems to be, now that the panic attack's passed." Dan studied Rik as if trying to figure out what to do with him. "I think it would still be a good idea if he saw a doctor sometime soon, but honestly, I don't think it's an emergency at this point, and I think the ED would be the wrong environment for him."

Meaning the noise and chaos might set off another panic attack. One look at Bonnie's face told Marco she'd come to the same conclusion as him.

He stroked Rik's hair and kissed the top of his head, trying to soothe away some of the building tightness in Rik's body. "Is it okay to take him home?"

"No!" Rik's head came up, clipping Marco's chin. He stared at Marco with eyes so wide Marco could almost see a rim of bloodshot whites around the blue. "Don't leave me. Please don't leave me up there."

If Marco's heart hadn't already dissolved into a Rik-shaped puddle, that would've done it. He raked his fingers through Rik's hair and kissed his cheek. "Don't worry, babe. I'm not letting you out of my sight. Either I'm staying with you at the estate, or you're staying with me at my place, but there's no way in hell I'm leaving you alone."

Rik's stare didn't waver, but the budding fear leached away. "I don't want to go back to the estate. I want to stay with you."

Marco smiled. He wondered if Rik even realized what a huge step forward he'd just taken.

Dan cleared his throat. "To answer your question, yeah, I

think it's fine to take him on home. I'm not a doctor, Henrik, but as far as I can tell you're perfectly healthy."

"Okay." Rik stirred, sat up straight and looked at Dan, the women whose name they'd never asked and the other couple of firefighters standing around watching them. "Thank you for helping me. All of you."

A calendar-boy smile spread over Dan's face. "No problem, man. I'm glad you're okay."

"Absolutely." The woman started forward, seemed to think better of it, and gave him a wave instead. "Take it easy. And take care of yourself."

The other men all murmured similar things as Marco helped Rik stand and they left the station arm in arm. Bonnie stayed behind to talk to the group. She came jogging back to the car just as Marco was buckling Rik into the passenger seat. She raised her eyebrows. Marco shook his head.

"Is he really okay?" she asked as Marco crossed in front of the car on his way to the driver's seat. "I can't imagine he enjoys being treated like a child."

"He doesn't, no. But he wasn't buckling the seat belt, so what was I supposed to do?" Marco glanced at Rik through the windshield. "I know what you mean, though. Normally, he'd give me hell for doing that shit, but he didn't say a word. It worries me."

"Well, he's had a very traumatic experience today. He's probably exhausted, mentally and physically, and not thinking straight." Bonnie took Marco's hands in hers and gave them a squeeze. "I'll call Pierre to come get me. You take Rik straight home."

"No, sis, I can take you. It's not far."

She smiled. "That's sweet of you, but I'm not sure how your guy is going to react to having me in the car. He won't want to start panicking again, and he won't mean to, but he can't necessarily control his reactions. And he's especially vulnerable right now."

Knowing Rik, he'd feel guilty and miserable for having an attack in front of Bonnie. Marco would do anything to avoid that.

"I guess you're right." Marco let out a soft laugh. "Sorry, Bonnie."

"Don't worry about it. The guys said I could hang out here until Pierre comes to get me." Rising on tiptoe, she kissed his cheek. "Whatever happens, I'm so happy we're a family again, Marco."

His throat went tight. "Me too." He gathered her into his arms for a tight hug. "I'll call you, okay?"

"Okay." When he let her go, she headed back to the station with a smile and a wave. "Talk to you later."

Turning back to the car, he opened the driver's side door and slid behind the wheel. When he reached over to tuck Rik's hair behind his ear, Rik finally met his gaze. Rik's face radiated sadness, but he no longer looked ready to jump and run.

Marco traced the line of Rik's jaw with his fingertips. "It'll be okay."

The sorrow didn't leave Rik's eyes, but the corners of his mouth turned up just a little. It was better than nothing.

§ § §

Henrik called Gus on the way to Marco's apartment. He had to admit he was happy to get her voice mail instead of having to talk to her directly. She'd be furious with him. He told her he was fine, he was with Marco and not to worry, though he knew she would. He promised to call her the next morning and hung up, hoping she wouldn't have a meltdown.

Marco didn't say a word, just patted Henrik's knee in silent sympathy. The gesture made him feel better.

Marco's apartment over Furnace Glassworks was small, old and cluttered, but Henrik liked it right away. It had a bright, creative feel that gave him a sense of instant calm, in spite of the beat-up furniture and the scarred floor. He figured that probably had a lot to do with the artwork scattered all over the room, art he instantly recognized as Marco's—metal sculptures, delicate glass creations, even a few pieces of pottery.

"I love your place." Henrik wandered over to a book shelf crowded with more glass bottles than books. He picked up a tiny cup fashioned from emerald green glass blown paper thin. "These are beautiful. It amazes me how you can make things like this."

"Thanks. I can't *not* do it. That shit keeps me sane." Marco switched on the lamp beside the sofa, then went to Henrik and put both arms around him from behind. "You want me to fix you something to eat?"

"No, thanks. I'm not hungry." Henrik turned in Marco's arms and wound his arms around Marco's neck. "Thank you for letting me stay here."

"Like there was any way I would've said no." Marco studied Henrik with transparent worry. "Are you sure you'll be okay here? It's not bothering you to be away from home?"

Henrik shook his head. "You know how much I hate the retreats. And your apartment is great. It *feels* like home to me." He pressed closer and rubbed his cheek against Marco's. The stubble scratched his skin, sending a pleasurable shiver down his spine. "That's probably weird, but I suppose it's hardly the weirdest thing about me."

"It's not *weird*. It's just one more thing that makes you interesting." Marco cupped Henrik's butt in one hand. He lifted the other hand and slid it through Henrik's hair, massaging his scalp. "I hate hearing you put yourself down like that."

Henrik laughed in spite of everything. "I'm only telling the truth as I see it."

"Yeah, well, I think your vision of yourself is distorted." Marco drew back enough to look Henrik in the eye. "What made you decide to come down the mountain?"

Maybe the question shouldn't have irritated Henrik, considering how Marco had come to his rescue today, but it did.

He didn't know how to answer honestly without sounding like he blamed Marco, when in fact he laid the blame for what happened squarely on himself, where it belonged.

He grasped Marco's shoulders and fought to hold his gaze. "I just wanted to be with you. I thought if I could make it down here to see you, then—" He stopped before he could say anything too revealing.

Marco, of course, saw right through him. "Jesus Christ, Rik." Letting go of Henrik, Marco crossed to the window overlooking the street and plopped onto the threadbare sofa underneath it. "You really thought you had to put yourself through that for me to think you're, what, important? Worthy of my attention?" He shook his head. "You're something else."

This time, it didn't sound like a compliment. Henrik turned around, pretending to inspect the shelf full of artwork again. "It was a stupid thing to do. I know that."

"Yeah, it was. Don't you know by now how important you are to me?"

Something caught hard in Henrik's chest. A bittersweet brew of conflicting emotions propelled him across the floor to stand in front of Marco, heart racing and a confused jumble of words all fighting to get out at once.

"Oh, yes. Nothing says *you're important to me* like canceling the one most important weekend *ever* at the last minute." Henrik crossed his arms, frowning. He wasn't sure he'd made a lot of sense, but he thought Marco understood.

Sure enough, Marco slumped forward, elbows on his knees. "I know. You're right. Bonnie said the same thing."

"I know. I was there."

Marco shot him a sharp glare. "You're not gonna cut me any breaks at all, are you?"

Henrik raised his eyebrows. "Should I?"

"No, I guess not." Marco's mouth twisted into a wry smile. "Will you sit down? So we can talk like a couple of civilized people?"

The desire to be close to Marco won out over Henrik's anger. He sat.

Marco took his hand and held on tight. "I see what you're saying. I never should've canceled this weekend. And this isn't the first time I've canceled on you either. I'm sorry. You're right, I can hardly expect you to know what I'm thinking when I do shit like that."

Part of Henrik wanted to deny that Marco was in the wrong, if only to take the regret out of his eyes. Because, really, *had* he done anything wrong? "You probably had legitimate reasons to cancel, so it's hard for me to sit in judgment. But yeah, I'll admit it hurt, and it made me question whether I was as important to you as you are to me."

Marco scrunched his nose as if the thought caused him physical pain. "Okay, I have to come clean here. Most of the time, I really did cancel for the reasons I said I did. Running this shop is a lot of work, and I have to spend time making more stuff now and then if I want to keep it going. Plus the creative side of it is what I love about it, you know? But a couple of times, I only canceled because I needed to be alone. I needed to think." He glanced up at Henrik, his expression miserable. "I was scared. Which doesn't excuse me being a lying prick, but there it is."

Okay, *that* felt like a kick in the teeth. Henrik pulled his hand from Marco's, leaned against the back of the sofa and stared at the ceiling. "You're a bastard."

"I know."

Henrik wished the anguish in Marco's voice didn't get to him, but it did. "Stop sounding sorry. I don't want to feel bad for you."

"But I *am* sorry." The couch cushions shifted as Marco moved. His face came into view, looking gutted. "I had a lot of doubts, Rik. But I tell you something. When that fireman answered your phone, every doubt I ever had went flying out the window. I realized I don't ever want to be with anyone else, and I don't ever want to be without you."

God, if Marco meant what Henrik thought he did…

Still, he found he couldn't simply accept Marco's declaration of undying devotion without making damn sure he wouldn't lie again to avoid being with Henrik. He didn't think he'd survive that.

Henrik peered into Marco's wide, anxious eyes with as much calm as he could manage. "I want that too. But can you handle being with someone like me? Because I think today just proved that I'm not ever going to be normal."

Relief relaxed Marco's features. "I know what your problems are, and I can deal with them. I'll help you. We'll work through everything together."

He was sincere, Henrik knew, but… "Relationships don't come with a guarantee, Marco. You can't give me that, no matter how much you might want to. And I'm not sure I could take it if I had you in my life, then you changed your mind and left me. That probably makes me weak, but it's how I feel."

Marco's brows drew together in the stubborn expression Henrik had seen many times before. "I'm already in your life. And that's where I want to stay."

Henrik took a deep breath and made himself say the words he wasn't entirely sure he believed. "I don't know if you should."

Marco stared at him. The dark eyes narrowed. "But you want me to."

Henrik looked away. "That's beside the point. You—"

"Shut up."

Incredulous, Henrik gaped at Marco. "What? You can't—"

"Goddammit, shut *up*." To Henrik's shock, Marco clamped a hand over Henrik's mouth. Silenced more from sheer surprise than anything else, Henrik stared at Marco. Marco glowered back, brow furrowed and dark eyes snapping with anger, worry, frustration and something else, something that made Henrik's heart beat faster.

"That's better." Marco shifted closer, his fingers digging into

Henrik's cheeks. "I swear to Christ, you're the most irritating man on the fucking planet." He sighed, shoulders slumping. He looked so tired and defeated that Henrik elected to sit still and listen instead of shoving him away. "Yeah, sure, it's work dealing with your issues. It's not always easy being with you. And, yeah, maybe I could find somebody else who didn't have all the baggage. Who was just average." Marco dropped his hand from Henrik's mouth. His gaze held Henrik's, full of an apprehension Henrik felt all the way to his core. "But he wouldn't be you. Nobody could ever be you, and that just would not work for me." Marco bit his lip, lifted his hand and touched Henrik's cheek as if he wasn't sure whether or not he was allowed to. "I love you."

Love. Not a word Henrik had ever dreamed of hearing directed at him from anyone but Gus, in anything more than a sisterly way. He'd have believed himself to be dreaming now, if it weren't for the drone of Marco's ancient refrigerator and the sharp scent of fear-sweat from his shirt.

Fear caused by Henrik. Because of his panic attack, something Gus had seen more than once but Marco hadn't. Well, technically he still hadn't seen it, but he'd seen the results of it, and it had obviously frightened him. Henrik thought anyone would find such a thing disturbing, but to see someone you love suffering such a thing must be terrible. He knew he'd rather endure the worst tortures imaginable than for Marco to go through even one bad panic attack.

Overcome by a complex swell of emotions, Henrik cupped Marco's face in both palms and kissed him, putting everything he'd felt and denied for months into the press of his lips and the stroke of his tongue. Marco let out a soft, helpless noise. He pulled Henrik up to straddle his lap, both arms snug around Henrik's waist, hands spread on his back. To Henrik, nothing had ever felt so good. Not even the first time they made love.

Eventually, Henrik broke the kiss and rested his forehead against Marco's. "I love you too. Just in case you didn't know." Marco laughed, and Henrik grinned. The rush of it all kicked his heartbeat into a gallop fast enough to make him dizzy.

Marco loved him. Really, truly loved him, in spite of all the difficulties and restrictions that went along with loving someone like him.

Closing his eyes, Henrik buried his face in the curve of Marco's neck and breathed deep, smelling sweat and skin and a whiff of Marco's soap. As usual, the scent—all male, all Marco—sent the blood rushing into Henrik's crotch and formed a pool of heat in his belly. Pressing closer, he planted open-mouthed kisses on the spot where the pulse jumped in Marco's throat.

He got a low, sweet groan in response. Marco slid both hands up Henrik's back under his T-shirt. "Take this off."

Henrik sat back long enough to pull off his shirt and throw it on the floor. He set to work unbuttoning Marco's shirt, opened it and bent to suck one brown nipple into his mouth. Marco arched against his mouth, both hands tangled in his hair.

Smiling against Marco's chest, Henrik dug his teeth into Marco's nipple and tugged for a moment before letting go. "Where's your bed? Or do you sleep out here?"

"Naw, I got a bedroom." Marco pulled Henrik's head up by the hair and kissed him hard. "Get up."

Henrik scrambled off Marco's lap, and yelped when Marco smacked him on the ass. Grinning, he reached for Marco's hand. Marco took it, linking their fingers, and led Henrik to one of two doors on the other side of the room, in the opposite corner from the tiny kitchen.

The bedroom was plain, but functional. The double bed was tucked into the corner under a small window that overlooked the alley behind the shop. A sturdy antique wooden dresser and mirror stood opposite the bed. The narrow closet opened beside the dresser. A wooden table sat beside the bed. Next to the door, a tall bookshelf overflowed with books of all types.

Henrik liked it immediately. He let go of Marco's hand and put both arms around his neck. "I'm glad I'm here."

"Me too." Marco stroked his cheek, brown eyes full of a tender light. "Take off those jeans, beautiful. It's been way too long since I've seen you naked."

Heart pounding, Henrik stepped back, toed off his running shoes and skinned out of his jeans. He left them in a heap on the floor so he could go back to Marco and free his erection from the snug black denim.

Marco moaned when Henrik pushed his jeans and underwear down to his thighs and curled a hand around his cock. "God, babe."

Sinking to his knees, Henrik took Marco into his mouth, swallowing Marco's thick length until the head hit the back of his throat and cut off his breath. The almost-gag was worth it for the way Marco gasped his name like a prayer and fisted both hands in his hair.

Marco did that every time, but Henrik never got tired of it. Knowing he could make Marco feel that good gave him an incredible sense of power.

Just as Henrik tasted the tang of pre-come on his tongue, Marco tugged on his hair. "Stop. Gonna come."

Henrik pulled off and sat back on his heels. Not that he didn't like it when Marco came in his mouth. He did, very much. But he wanted Marco inside him, and he wouldn't get that if Marco came now.

"Goddamn." Grinning, Marco held a hand down to help Henrik stand. "You have a natural talent at that."

Henrik laughed, breathless with the desire thumping through his veins. He let Marco pull him to his feet and straight into Marco arms. "Thanks. I learned from the best."

Marco's expression went soft and tender. "I've missed you so much."

All the things Henrik wanted to say got stuck in his suddenly-tight throat. He kissed Marco's lips, putting everything he felt into it. "I missed you too," he whispered when they broke apart. He walked backward, taking Marco with him, until his legs hit the mattress. He lay back on the mattress, watching Marco's gaze turn heavy. "Come to bed."

Marco struggled out of the shoes Henrik belatedly realized he was still wearing and the jeans and underwear that were tangled around his thighs, then crawled onto the bed on top of Henrik. They shared a slow, deep kiss that had Henrik arching upward in search of more contact.

"I got tested," Marco breathed, his lips still brushing Henrik's. "I'm negative, on all counts." He kissed Henrik again, a brief touch that made him ache for more. Digging his hands into Marco's ribs, he tilted his head and stole a harder, deeper kiss. Marco smiled, the smile that managed to be sweet and wicked at once, the one Henrik would give anything to see. "Wanna go bareback?"

Henrik had watched enough online porn to know what bareback meant. He didn't mind Marco using a condom, but the idea of Marco fucking him without one sent a luscious shudder through him. "Yeah. Let's do that."

The smile on Marco's face widened, lost its sweetness and turned one hundred percent sexy with a dash of evil. "Thought you might go for that." He tilted his head to mouth along Henrik's neck. Teeth dug into the skin of Henrik's shoulder, and he gasped. Marco let go and licked away the sting of the bite. "I can't wait to be inside you without a rubber, babe. To just feel you all around me with nothing in the way." He kissed Henrik's collarbone, his throat, the spot behind his ear that always gave him goose bumps. "I figure it'll be better than getting religion."

Henrik could only nod. He lifted his hips in a frantic bid to tell Marco what he wanted. His cock rubbed Marco's for a bright, brief moment. Henrik moaned.

Above him, Marco closed his eyes, lips parting in a soundless sigh. When his eyes opened again, his eyes glittered with the same need thumping through Henrik's veins. "Don't move."

Henrik moved while Marco fetched the lube from the bedside drawer, but only to spread his legs wide. Marco didn't mind, judging by the way his gaze raked over Henrik's body when he knelt, lube bottle in hand, between Henrik's sprawled thighs.

I get to see him look at me like that for the rest of our lives. The thought nearly stopped Henrik's breath with its power.

He pulled one leg up to his chest, watching Marco's face that whole time. "Come on, Marco."

Marco laughed. It sounded breathless. "Yeah, yeah. Pushy."

Opening the lube, he poured some in his hand, closed the bottle and set it on the table again. He slicked his cock, then reached between Henrik's legs to rub the rest on his hole.

Henrik let out a low, broken noise when Marco pushed two fingers inside him. After the slight initial discomfort of the first couple of times, he'd learned to love this part—the first penetration by Marco's long, slim fingers, those clever artist's fingers that knew just how deep to go, just how to spread and stretch him, just where to press and rub to make him see stars. The sure, gentle way Marco prepared him was almost as good as Marco's cock inside him.

Almost.

Nothing, he thought as Marco spread him open and thrust home, *nothing* could compare to the feel of Marco's cock so deep inside his ass he could almost taste it, hammering his gland until he lost himself in bliss.

The head of Marco's prick dragged across his prostate. He let out a sob. "God. Marco." He clasped Marco close with arms and legs, his face buried in Marco's throat, and felt safe and loved and protected in the midst of the climax already building in his core.

"Yeah, babe." Marco braced an elbow beneath Henrik's shoulder, his hand buried in Henrik's hair as he loved to do during sex. He took Henrik's cock in his other hand and stroked him with the firm, just-this-side-of-rough touch he liked best. "Feels so fucking good."

Henrik agreed. In fact, he thought it felt even better than usual. Not because of the lack of a condom, but because Marco loved him. That certainty added an extra zing to every thrust of Marco's hips, every moan, every hitch of his breath and tightening of his fingers around Henrik's cock.

Nothing so physically intense could last long. Henrik's orgasm overtook him within minutes, shaking him like a toy and tearing a sharp cry from him. Marco held still, buried to the hilt in Henrik's ass. It took a dazed moment for him to realize Marco was coming too, spilling his spunk not into a latex sheath, but right into Henrik's body.

Knowing that gave Henrik a sense of intimacy stronger than any he'd ever known or imagined. Stripped emotionally bare and full to the brim with feelings too raw for words, he clung to Marco, caressing his back, his shoulders, the hair he kept so short it was almost nothing but stubble. He laid open-mouthed kisses on Marco's neck. The skin there tasted faintly salty with sweat. Henrik licked at Marco's pulse point, just because he could.

Marco hummed, lifted his head and kissed Henrik's chin. "You're a real cuddle-monster after sex, you know that?"

Henrik laughed, dislodging Marco's softened cock from inside him, along with a dribble of come. "Cuddle-monster? Did you really just say that?" He wriggled his hips, his legs still locked around Marco's waist. "Wow, I'm leaking."

"Yeah. It's a side effect of going bare. But it's not that bad." Grinning, Marco pecked Henrik on the lips. "And yes, I said it. You are a cuddle-monster."

Laughing again, Henrik framed Marco's face in his hands. "And you're nuts. But I like you anyway."

The teasing grin on Marco's face eased into a smile bright enough to light the world. "Well, good, because you're stuck with me."

"I like how that sounds. Come here."

Marco let Henrik guide him down into a deep, lazy kiss, the kind Henrik loved more than any other. As Marco's tongue slid against his, Henrik's happiness expanded inside him until he thought he might float away.

In the years since realizing why he panicked every time he tried to leave the estate, he'd come to terms with what that meant for his life. He'd resigned himself to living and dying alone. Then along came Marco. How Henrik had gotten lucky enough to find the one man willing to share his isolation and fill his days and nights with joy, he had no idea. But he knew a good thing when he had it in his hands. He intended to hang on to this one.

Epilogue

"Okay. Are you ready for this?"

In the passenger seat of Marco's car, Rik drew a couple of deep breaths, blowing them out in a slow stream. He nodded. "Yes. Let's go."

Marco studied Rik's white face and too-wide eyes with concern, but didn't ask. In the nine months they'd been together, he'd become well acquainted with Rik's stubborn streak, not to mention his iron will when he set his mind to something.

Like this whole going-to-town thing. Marco knew that when they first decided to commit to each other, Rik had expected him to become a hermit as well. Marco would've done it, gladly, as long as he could keep producing and selling his art. Before long, though, Rik got it into his head that Marco wouldn't be happy hidden away at the estate, even with the brand new hot shop he had built up there. So Rik came to Marco one day looking terrified but determined and announced that he was going to overcome his fear of going out in public, and Marco was going to help him.

Rik said he had his psychiatrist's blessing. Marco wouldn't have believed it if he hadn't asked. But he did, the good doctor confirmed it, and that was that.

The best part of that whole business was, in Marco's opinion, the agreement to occasional joint sessions with him and Rik. After all, he was a permanent part of Rik's life now. Might as well be part of his therapy, too.

Of course, the whole *I'm going down the mountain and you're helping me* business was when Marco learned there was no changing Rik's mind once he'd decided on something. Which was how they ended up here, on the street outside Marco's old apartment—Darryl had taken over the lease when Marco moved into the estate with Rik—all set to drive down Gatlinburg's main drag in broad daylight. They'd made the trip once late at night, and Marco had driven Rik through the back roads of the town a few times so he could get used to other cars on the road. This would be the first time Rik had ridden down the main road in daytime traffic since his childhood, though. Marco hoped he was really ready.

He'd already asked Marco to teach him to drive once he'd learned not to panic as a passenger. Marco didn't want to think that far ahead just yet.

"All right. Here we go." Marco cranked the engine, put the car in gear and pulled away from the curb.

When Marco first signed the lease for Furnace Glassworks' space, he hadn't much liked it being on a side street instead of the main road. Foot traffic meant business in a town like Gatlinburg. Now, however, he was glad of the few extra seconds it gave Rik to gather himself and prepare for the chaos that was the town's major artery, even on a Sunday morning.

"Turn left," Rik said when Marco flipped on his right turn signal.

Marco glanced at him. "I thought we'd try going away from the town center this first time. We can go through the thick of it next time."

Rik's fair brows pulled together. "Turn left. I'm feeling strong today, and I want to do this."

Shaking his head, Marco switched his turn signal to left. "You're the boss." The traffic light turned red as he approached. One more thing to be grateful for, in his opinion.

"I'm the boss. Yes. I'm in charge of this." Rik shut his eyes and breathed deep. His shoulders visibly relaxed when he breathed out. He opened his eyes and stared at the road ahead with single minded focus. "I can do this. My mind is stronger than my fear."

Life had taught Marco not to put much faith in such things, but it seemed to be working for Rik, so who was he to judge?

The light turned green. Marco shot Rik an encouraging smile. "All right, this is it. I'm going to drive until you tell me to stop.

Let me know when you need me to turn off."

Rik gave him a faint nod. Marco turned through the intersection and into the lighter than normal but still busy traffic of downtown Gatlinburg.

Beside him, Rik dug both hands into the worn vinyl seat and whispered encouragement to himself under his breath. His eyes stayed open, gaze darting back and forth between the shops on either side of the road and the stop-and-go crawl of vehicles traveling through the town. Marco clutched the wheel in a death grip and did his best to keep most of his attention on the road. He had to trust Rik to speak up if he felt a panic attack coming on. Marco causing a wreck because he was too busy watching Rik wouldn't help anybody.

They made it almost all the way through the town's central tourist district before Rik started to fidget in his seat. He shut his eyes tight. "Okay, I can't handle any more. Let's go back."

Marco didn't wait for a better route. He turned right at the next road and took the nearly deserted side road for a couple of miles before looping back to skirt around the town. He crossed the main road away from the center of the city and approached his shop from the other side.

The drive didn't last long, really, but it felt like forever. Rik sat in tense silence, eyes shut and fingers white-knuckled on the edge of his seat. His body didn't tremble like it had the first couple of times they'd driven in and around the town, though, which Marco took as measurable progress. Even better, when Marco parked the car in the alleyway behind Furnace Glassworks and Rik opened his eyes, Marco saw not a trace of fear or panic. Anxiety, sure. Rik wouldn't be human if he hadn't felt anxious about this adventure of theirs. But to take such a tremendous step, to conquer a lifetime of crippling terror, even for a few minutes… That was huge.

So full of pride he thought he might burst, Marco unbuckled his seat belt and threw both arms around Rik's neck. "You did it, Rik. You are a fucking *god*."

"I did it. I really did." Rik let out a shaky laugh. He looked at Marco, blue eyes bright and a wide smile on his face. "Maybe we can go out for dinner one day. That would be great, wouldn't it?"

"It would. I'd love to take you out someplace fancy and show you off." Cupping Rik's cheek in his palm, Marco leaned in to kiss him. Maybe it was his imagination, but he thought Rik's mouth tasted sweeter fresh off of his victory. "You want to go in with me to talk to Darryl?" His assistant had taken over most of the day-to-day running of the shop, leaving Marco free to create full-time. Gus had been good for Darryl that way, showing him that he had the chops to run the place without Marco's help. Everyone—Darryl, Marco, and Furnace Glassworks—had benefited as a result.

"I'd love to." Rik beamed like he did every time he went with Marco to Furnace. He'd only recently worked up to going inside the shop during business hours, and he still got a thrill out of it. "I think I'll get Gus a birthday present while I'm here."

"I keep telling you, you don't have to buy things. I'll make something for you." Marco climbed out of the car, keys in hand, and shut the door behind him.

Rik got out and circled the rear of the car. "I know. But I like to buy things at your shop. It makes me feel like a regular person." He took Marco's hand and peered at him with that gaze that seemed to see straight to his soul. "No one's ever made me feel normal before. That's what I love most about you."

As usual, the directness in Rik's eyes and in his words filled Marco with warmth. He kissed Rik's knuckles. "Nobody's ever made me feel special before, so I guess we're even."

Rik laughed. They headed for the shop entrance with their fingers entwined.

As a couple, Marco figured they had a ways to go, and Rik still had a lot to overcome. But Marco no longer harbored any doubts—about himself, about Rik or about the two of them. Whatever challenges they faced, they'd climb the mountain together, and come out on top.

About the Author

ALLY BLUE is acknowledged by the world at large (or at least by her heroes, who tend to suffer a lot) as the Popess of Gay Angst. She has a great big suggestively-shaped hat and rides in a bullet-proof Plexiglas bubble in Christmas parades. Her harem of manwhores does double duty as bodyguards and inspirational entertainment. Her favorite band is Radiohead, her favorite color is lime green and her favorite way to waste a perfectly good Saturday is to watch all three extended version LOTR movies in a row. Her ultimate dream is to one day ditch the evil day job and support the family on manlove alone. She is not a hippie or a brain surgeon, no matter what her kids' friends say.

Ally can be found on the internet at:

http://www.allyblue.com

Trademarks Acknowledgment

The author acknowledges the trademark status and trademark owners of the following wordmarks mentioned in this work of fiction:

Armani: Giorgio Armani S.P.A.

Bugs Bunny: Warner Bros.

Girl Scout: The Girls Scouts of the United States of America

iPhone: Apple, Inc.

Super Bowl: NFL Enterprises

Xanax: The Upjohn Company

CPSIA information can be obtained at www.ICGtesting.com
Printed in the USA
BVOW02s2357221213

339794BV00001B/19/P